Nau

W9-CAB-838

Nightwood

NightWood

Patricia Windsor

Delacorte Press

Published by Delacorte Press
an imprint of Random House Children's Books
a division of Random House, Inc.
New York

Delacorte Press and colophon are registered trademarks of Random House, Inc.

www.randomhouse.com/teens

Educators and librarians, for a variety of teaching tools,
visit us at www.randomhouse.com/teachers

Library of Congress Cataloging-in-Publication Data

Windsor, Patricia.
Nightwood / Patricia Windsor. — 1st ed.
p. cm.
Summary: Eleven teenagers' lives intertwine during their separate outings and turn into a nightmare as they flee from a hideous monster.
ISBN-13: 978-0-385-73312-0 (tr) — ISBN-13: 978-0-385-90331-8 (glb)
ISBN-10: 0-385-73312-7 (tr) — ISBN-10: 0-385-90331-6 (glb)
[1. Cannibalism—Fiction. 2. Horror stories—Fiction.] I. Title.
PZ7.W7245Ni 2006
[Fic]—dc22   2006012407

The text of this book is set in 12-point Minion.

Printed in the United States of America

10 9 8 7 6 5 4 3 2 1

First Edition

To Richard Hampton, with love and thanks

HE COMES FROM THE WOOD, DARK, WALKING BETWEEN
  THE TREES,
INTO THE HEART AND SOUL OF ME, UNINVITED,
LODGING THERE, DELIGHTED . . .

from "Damaged Goods" by Sybil Eliot
In the Trees, *1955*

PART ONE

Saturday

CHAPTER 1

He ran at night and hid by day, crawling into dark places that were a little too much like his old lair—but then, it was only the familiar that could make you feel really safe.

He thought he could run until he was dead; there was nothing to hold him back. He'd run until his flesh dropped off and the wind and rain polished his bones. The house was far behind. But how far was far enough?

I am . . . I am . . . He ran chanting, trying to remember his rightful name. Never to be called *Boy* anymore. He held on to that little frayed string of hope that he could change what had been born into him, put a stop to the twenty-four-hour picture show going on in his head. But maybe that was like hoping he could stop breathing, smelling, eating. Was it possible to change a taste for blood?

He had been running south, through a landscape of old farms, shanties and trailers, startled by the hulks of rusting cars sitting like giant rats in the moonlight, avoiding the lonely lights in bedroom windows, trembling at the sudden howl of an edgy hound. Keeping to the county roads. He was always lonely at night. Daddy had liked the highways. *Get the best girlies hitchhiking on them,* he had said. *Fresh meat.*

Now the sun was coming up and he was tired. A sign at a crossroads said HATTON 5 MI. DELONGA 8 MI. He was getting close to towns. Ahead he could smell a swampy area. Nobody would be walking through there. The place had a mean, bad look; the kind of place that knew him. Old cypress trees stood on their knees in murky water, their branches draped with shawls of moss. He felt his way between the tupelos and black gum trees, his brown, cracked feet trailing slimy duckweed as he waded through inky pools. This was where he belonged, low and deep, down in the rot-stinking mud, down with the snake-headed skinks, with bottom-feeders and cottonmouths.

People were scared of the swamp, worried about snakes, about being gored by wild pigs.

But no harm would come to him here. The swamp creatures recognized him by his smell, saw into the darkness of his heart and knew him for what he was: one of their kind. He would hide here until dark. Then he'd run again.

CHAPTER 2

The little Honda Civic looked like a red ant moving between the SUVs and long-haul trucks on the highway. Gena sat in the backseat, listening to Casey and Maryann talking and laughing up front, feeling like a third wheel. Feeling carsick too. Though maybe it wasn't so much being carsick as thinking about what she was doing. Riding off to some town she'd never heard of instead of sitting on the bus with the rest of the class on their way to Washington, D.C. How did she get herself into this? Not really a hard question—she knew the answer. By telling a lie.

"How're you doing back there?" Casey asked, half turning around, blowing cigarette smoke into the backseat and interrupting Gena's quiet agony.

"I'm fine." Gena's voice sounded small and unsure, but she couldn't get up the energy to be perky right now.

Casey and Maryann were the ultimate in perky. Maryann was swigging Coke out of a can; Casey, holding her cigarette out the window, taking her hand off the wheel to punch in a new station on the radio. They were probably sorry they asked her to come. It was beyond her how they didn't feel guilty like she did.

Gena kept envisioning her mother phoning the hotel and finding out she wasn't there. Or the school bus crashing and everyone getting killed. Gena would still be alive and the lie would be more than obvious. It was such a stupid idea, she almost laughed.

Maryann turned around.

"I was just thinking about my mother," Gena mumbled, trying to cover her anxiety.

"Right," Maryann said, giving her a look.

But Gena wasn't about to tell them she felt guilty. They seemed to be immune to guilt. They hadn't even cared when they were all dragged in by the principal and almost suspended. Maryann said that her father didn't care about anything except that she made dinner and cleaned the house, and Casey's parents were always at the country club or some fund-raiser. Gena sort of envied that they had the freedom to do what they wanted. Her mother was always on her case. Ironically, now that she was free it didn't feel so great. The truth was, she had actually wanted to go on the class trip. But everything got so mixed up after the three of them got in trouble.

The worst guilt was about the pizza party. She had felt like crying then, and she still did when she thought of it. Her mother and Matt, ordering pizza, decorating the kitchen, giving her a bon voyage party. And Matt asking her to bring him a souvenir back from D.C. How in the world was she going to manage that? Finding a souvenir of the nation's capital in a cabin in the woods?

It had all started in science lab with Casey wanting to make a smoke bomb.

"All we need is sugar and potassium nitrate," Casey said, like she made them every day.

Maryann looked in the supply cabinets. "No sugar."

"Okay, we'll bring some tomorrow." Casey was clearly in charge—the next thing she was taking a cigarette out of her backpack and lighting it.

"You can't smoke in here!" Gena exclaimed, shocked.

"Chill out! I'm not going to *smoke* it." Grinning, she went over to the microwave and placed the cigarette on a glass slide. "Get me a cup of water, okay?"

Like the drone she had become, Gena fetched the water, then watched as Casey put the cup into the microwave along with the slide. "Watch this."

She tapped the buttons, the microwave started, and suddenly balls of orange light were jumping around inside. It looked awesome, but Gena was sure something was going to blow up.

"Where'd you learn that?" Maryann demanded as soon as the microwave dinged. It was clear she wanted to try it herself.

"On the Internet." Casey was smug. "If you think

that was good, bring some old CDs tomorrow. I'll show you something that will really blow your mind."

While the possibilities of danger didn't seem to bother them, Gena could only think of twisted metal and burning hair. Typical.

They were in the lab after school that day because they had been given detention for not completing their experiment in class. The three of them were lab partners. Casey and Maryann talked and fooled around most of the time while Gena tried to get the assignments done. But that day they just kept talking and telling jokes and Gena couldn't concentrate. So when the bell rang and the lab wasn't done, they were all in trouble.

Casey and Maryann had known each other like forever. Gena had the bad luck to transfer schools halfway through the term and didn't know anybody. When she'd been assigned to them in lab, she naturally felt like a third wheel, but they were friendly enough and even made her their partner in a project for history class. It felt nice having instant friends, even though she suspected they might be a little wilder than she was.

Gradually she got to know them better. She felt sorry for Maryann because she didn't have a mother, only a father who was a slob who drank all the time and bossed her around. She was in awe of Casey, who lived in one of the town's gated subdivisions. Her parents had wanted her to go to a private school, but she insisted on attending the public high school. "Because they hate it," Casey said.

Being with each of them alone was better than seeing

them together. They had a history and inside jokes, and when the three of them were together, Casey and Maryann talked about things Gena didn't know anything about. It took awhile before she realized they didn't care if they got into trouble. Which was why they got detention and had to make up the lab. But instead of making up the work, Casey did her thing with her cigarette in the microwave so they got stuck with another afternoon in lockdown, to which Maryann brought a couple of CDs she didn't want.

Like a bad dream that wouldn't go away, the next day was a repeat performance, only worse. At first, when Casey put the CDs into the microwave, they were looking at a sparkling blue light show. It was really beautiful, almost mesmerizing, and they just stood there watching the sparks dancing around inside the oven. Then the microwave started to smoke and there was the most horrible smell. They turned it off and opened the door and started fanning the air, but the whole room reeked.

So Casey came up with a solution. They'd make a smoke bomb spiked with cinnamon gum to kill the smell of the burned CD. Except the supposedly small smoke bomb erupted into a volcano, filled up the lab and blew out into the hall. The fire alarm went off, teachers came running and that was when the real trouble began.

The principal said they would be suspended. Gena was mortified when her mother actually called the man and begged him to change the punishment, even cried to him about it. In the end, nothing huge happened because of something Casey's father said to the principal. Their punishment was to stay after school for a week sorting stuff for a jumble sale to raise money for a new gym. Gena thought it was a minor penalty until she started going through people's old junk. Some of the clothes stank, sorting the books into categories gave her a headache and the toys were sticky from little kids' spit and who knew what else.

On the third afternoon of sorting, they got to talking about the school trip. As usual, Casey's opinion was clear. "Are you kidding? Walking around museums all day and having chaperones watching your every move? I'm not signing up."

And just as predictably, Maryann was her flunky. "I wasn't going to go either," she admitted. "But I sort of got into some problems at the mall. And my dad, well, it would be better if I could just not be here for a while."

Gena opened her mouth but nothing came out. She was wondering what she could say that wouldn't sound as lame as the truth: she didn't have the money for the trip. But the truth popped out anyway. She felt herself going red. She knew Casey wouldn't comprehend how money could be a problem. There was never enough money for anything since the divorce. Gena was sick of hearing about it.

Then Casey said, "I have an idea. Let's all sign up and then go somewhere else."

"Like where?" Maryann asked.

"Like my parents' cabin in Delonga. We'll stay away for the whole week and our parents will think we're on the trip."

Maryann's face lit up. "Brilliant! What do you think, Gena?"

Gena didn't know how she could make herself any clearer. "I already told you. I don't have enough money."

"But that's the point!" Casey replied, with a wicked smile. "We won't really be going."

"But Casey," Maryann protested, "what would her mother think? That she can go for free? She'll have to pretend to sign up *and* pay the fee."

"And that leaves me out," Gena concluded, feeling sort of relieved.

Still Casey was insistent. "No problem, I'll give you the money."

Gena sighed. They just didn't understand. "My mother will wonder where it came from. She'll ask a lot of questions. She won't like me borrowing money."

Maryann interupted again. "So can't you get a job? Babysitting or something?"

At the time, Gena had felt a thrill of excitement, like going with them instead of the school trip just *might* be possible. She had never done anything like that before, and she hadn't stopped to think about whether going with Casey and Maryann was good or bad. She even forgot the reason she had ended up with them sorting junk every afternoon in the first place. At that moment, getting away for a week—if she could get away with it— had seemed like a great idea.

Or maybe it had been because she was sick of feeling like a stray dog since they moved there. Starting a new school halfway through her junior year had been hard. Everything about it was different. Everybody already had their friends and groups. She went home every day the first week and cried in her room at how shitty life was. All her mom did was keep saying "It'll be all right" and "You'll make new friends soon." Like life was a TV show. Her mother had no idea what school was like.

The prospect of doing something wild with Casey and Maryann had made Gena feel like she finally had friends of her own. You wouldn't ask someone you didn't trust to keep a secret like that, would you? You wouldn't ask someone you didn't like to spend a week with you in some cabin in the woods.

Suddenly, it was like a bright light appeared in her mind and she'd told them, "Maybe. Okay. I can offer to sit the kids on my street. Their mother is always trying to find a sitter."

And when she explained to her mother about earning money for the class trip, her Mom's face had softened. "All right, if it means that much to you."

So right away, Gena started feeling guilty because her mother was being nice, but she went ahead and got the babysitting job anyway. They were the kids from hell, but she put up with them. In fact, it was better that they were so awful and the job was so hard, because it made it seem like she was paying her dues for lying. On the last day of the ordeal, the kids' mother gave her an extra tip and told her to buy something nice for herself in Washington. Gena came home to a dark house and silence, and when she put on the kitchen light, her mom and Matt yelled "Surprise!" They'd set the table like a party and presented her with an instant camera to take pictures of the Capitol and the White House and the Washington Monument. She'd have to say she lost the camera.

She had been swept along until here she was, in the backseat of Casey's car, on her way to a place called Delonga, which Casey said was stone country, whatever that meant. When they had piled their stuff into the back, Gena noticed two big gallon jugs of white wine. Casey said she just called the liquor store and had it delivered along with the rest of the order her parents always placed. That gave Gena a sliver of doubt about what she was getting into. But it was too late. She couldn't turn back now.

CHAPTER 3

Maryann was replaying the scene with her father in her head. She'd been in her room trying on jeans—three new pairs—checking herself out in the mirror. You couldn't go by sizes. She'd made sure to take all sixes, but you wouldn't know it—one pair was way too tight, another was baggy. She was lucky to get one decent pair out of the haul.

"I gotta stop doing this," she said to herself as she stood there in front of the mirror tacked to the back of her bedroom door.

It had been hairy. She was sure she would have been stopped if it hadn't been for some mother screaming she'd lost her kid. That guy in the uniform had been eyeing her, but thankfully had to go check out the woman. Maryann felt like running, but she forced herself to look casual, walking only a little faster than normal, as if she had some important shopping to finish. She looked at her watch, put on a hassled expression. When she got outside to the parking lot, she ran like hell across the mall boulevard and into the Kroger, where she walked up and down the aisles awhile, just in case the security guy remembered and was looking around for her in the parking lot. Then she bought a soda and a candy bar, paid for it of course, and went out to wait for the bus.

And after all that, only one pair of jeans fit. She'd have to throw the others away. She couldn't risk selling them; it would be too much of a hassle anyway.

That was when her father's voice blasted her back into reality. "Maryann! We gonna eat tonight or what?"

Welcome to my life, she thought as she appraised herself in the mirror. She was rolling the other jeans up to put them into a plastic garbage bag when her father came up the stairs and started banging on the door. Usually it was locked, but he'd been passed out in front of the TV when she came in and she figured he wouldn't wake up for hours. Big mistake. When the door flew open, he looked as surprised as she was. Generally he had to shake the knob and bang and kick, then finally go away.

Immediately, his eyes fixed on the jeans.

"Whaddya doing? What's that?" He grabbed a pair out of the bag she was holding and looked at the price tag. "Where'd you get the money for this shit?"

"I had it, okay?"

"Yeah? Where's the tickets?"

He meant the receipts. She just looked at him and said nothing.

"You had it like hell. I know what you been doing, Maryann. Think I'm stupid? I seen the other stuff you brought in here."

He was bluffing, she thought. "You did? So why didn't you say something then?"

He got this nasty grin on his face. " 'Cause I'm a kindhearted guy? 'Cause I figured maybe you won the lottery? I'm tired of this shit."

"What's it to you?" she screamed at him. She shouldn't have. Better to have humored him and maybe he would have forgotten after eating supper and downing few beers.

"Oh? You think I want to see my daughter in jail?"

"Why should you care? You've been there yourself." That was another big mistake. He didn't like to be reminded. He liked to pretend he was one of the good guys.

"You shut yer face!" he yelled, and raised his hand to hit her. She'd been slapped by him before and she wasn't going to let it happen again. Walk around with a mark on her face, a black eye or something. They'd ask all those questions in school.

This time, she wasn't putting up with it. She backed up, grabbed the lamp from her dresser and threw it at him.

Not that it really hurt him or anything. But again, it was the wrong move. He got icily calm. Started talking in a low, creepy voice. "Hit your own father, huh? Know what I'm thinking? I'm thinking that I might call the cops on you, Maryann. You're not getting away with your thieving anymore. I turned my head once, but not again. This time, you're in trouble, little lady."

She was sure he wouldn't really do it. He didn't want anything to do with the law. But he was nasty enough to do something that would land her in trouble, and it scared her. She started thinking about leaving for a while—at least until he forgot it. He did that a lot, forgot why he was mad. She considered going on the class trip. But Casey's idea was better. It solved her problem perfectly.

CHAPTER 4

As she drove, Casey thought about Lane. He was the reason they were going to Delonga. It was the opportunity she had been praying for and it just about fell into her lap. She'd been at the country club with her parents when she first saw him, at one of those Sunday brunches that she only liked to go to because her dad let her have a Bloody Mary. Lane worked with the crew keeping up the lawns and flowers. A hottie to say the least. When she first saw him he was walking around with his shirt off, his jeans sitting just below his navel, his long blond hair turning platinum in the sun. And later that day, when she tried to talk to him, he almost backed away, like she would bite. He was all polite and stupid-acting; she almost expected him to tip his hat if he'd had one on. She figured he wasn't supposed to talk to the members, just act invisible. But Lane was anything but invisible.

The next time she saw him she actually got him to acknowledge she was alive. He even smiled. But he still looked nervous. That passed pretty quickly when she took him around to the back of the garages. They shared a cigarette, and by the time it burned down they understood each other. She kissed him long and hard before she went back to the club.

She gave him her address and cell phone number and told him how he could get into the subdivision without going past the guards, but he never called and never came around. She figured he was shy, or maybe just conditioned to think she was one of the untouchables, especially after her mother saw her walking across the lawn with him, holding on to his arm, and threw a fit. He'd told her later he was afraid he'd lose his job.

But he was always hanging behind the garage when she was at the club. He knew her car, and her parents' car, and they had an unspoken arrangement. It wasn't enough, though. She wondered how they could be alone together and that got her thinking about the class trip. What if she pretended to her parents that she was going but spent a week with Lane instead?

When she told him the idea he wasn't enthusiastic. He made excuses. "I got a job here," he said. "I can't be going off for a week."

"Well, what about a weekend?" she suggested. "You

must get some time off." She'd figure out a way to spend the weekend with him and then crash at a friend's house until the class came back from their trip. But when she told him the dates the class would be away he shook his head.

"That's when I'm going up to the lake fishing with my buddies."

She winced when she thought how close she had come to losing the chance to be with him. What if she had just accepted his excuse and left it at that? If she hadn't asked him that one crucial question, she would have lost the chance to be with him. Two words: "What lake?" And when he answered she could hardly believe it. Lane and his buddies were going to Delonga. She had to work hard to control her excitement and sound casual.

"Really? My parents have a cabin there. I could ride up to see you."

He looked sheepish. "I'm going with the guys, Casey. Jeff and Bailey and me. It's a fishing trip."

She put on a pout. "So you won't even think of sneaking out one night to meet me? When your buddies are asleep?"

"Naw, I don't think so. Really. Casey, you could get me in some serious trouble."

As hard as she had tried not to show her excitement, she then had to cover up the hurt of being blown off in favor of his friends. Jeff and Bailey, he said. Two of them and Lane made three. Which made her start thinking about Maryann and Gena. Two of them and her made three. A perfect equation. If she arrived at the lake with dates for his buddies, there wouldn't be a problem. No way they'd refuse to party. They'd probably have beer and she'd bring the girls, and wine just in case.

When she heard that Maryann and Gena weren't real happy about going on the class trip, it was as if everything was meant to be. She didn't tell them the details or about the guys, though. Maryann had an attitude—probably from being around her asshole father. Gena was a little wimpy and had just about lost it when they were threatened with being suspended from school. Better to just take them up to the lake and then casually bump into the guys. It would all work out, and she'd have a chance to be really alone with Lane once and for all.

CHAPTER 5

The girls didn't notice the truck that had been following them since they left home. It was trying to tail them surreptitiously but not doing a very good job. Still, they had no reason to be suspicious. Their parents truly thought they were on their way to Washington, D.C. And except for Maryann's father, none of them owned a pickup truck. The one belonging to Maryann's dad was dark green with racing stripes on the side. The truck following them was white, rusty around the edges, and had a few dents here and there. The kind of truck you wouldn't look at twice.

Trash Macey wondered what the heck he was doing. It had seemed like a good idea, taking off after the Honda when he noticed Casey and her friends packing it up with a bunch of gear. He was out early because he'd lost his job the night before and had crashed on a friend's couch after getting totally drunk. Mr. Hilley, his boss, had accused him of putting his hand in the till. He hadn't done it, but he was the low man and it was easy to give him the shove. So he was out of work and feeling shitty, and when he saw Casey and her friends, he got curious and decided to follow. Nothing else to do. Only now they were miles from where they started and he had no idea where they were headed.

Casey was a world-class snob, but she was also really hot. The guys accused him of following her around like a lost dog. "She's a little out of your league, Macey. Give it up." He knew it was true. She wouldn't give him the time of day. He knew it, but he couldn't get her out of his system.

And he knew a few things about the chicks with her. The skinny one with the drape for hair, he'd seen her in the mall hoisting merchandise. He had to admire her style; she did it like a pro. She better watch it, though. They were putting in those hidden cameras everywhere—she'd get busted eventually. The other one with the curly hair he didn't really know. New in school this year, looked like a scared mouse most of the time. Probably would wet her pants if you said boo.

Casey was the one for him. She lived at the Pointe in a big-ass house. He knew all about it from when he'd worked the summer before on the trash truck. They had a gate with a guard who checked your name and asked who you were going to see. That was a mistake—thinking everybody had to arrive in a car. Like nobody could come through the woods on foot. He'd done it hundreds of times. He'd found Casey's house and watched her through the window. She never suspected he was out there, in the tree, looking at her in her underwear.

He checked his gas gauge. He might have to fill up. They hadn't stopped yet and for the life of him he couldn't figure out where they were going. He always thought girls had to stop to pee a lot, but apparently he was wrong. Still, they'd have to stop sooner or later. He hoped it would be sooner.

Now that he had gone so far, he had no intention of giving up and turning back. He planned to follow them however far they went. Long as they stopped somewhere, for gas and a pee. He could use a Coke and a pee himself.

CHAPTER 6

Ben Jay knew his father would be in Linda's diner, eating his way through his usual lunch of beans and rice, corn bread and banana pudding. He also knew his father hated to be bothered at a meal. And usually there would be no reason for it. As his dad always said, nothing ever happened in Delonga, not even a traffic violation worth speaking of. Sometimes tourists fell into the lake, but so far nobody had drowned. But now, his father was finally going to get something to sink his teeth into—just like he was always hoping for.

Bursting into the diner, out of breath, he didn't even stop to shut the door behind him.

"Dad!" he yelled, skidding to a stop at the table.

The sheriff was sitting in his favorite booth near the back, giving him a view of the main street and the rest of the diner. He looked up from his plate.

"What in hell is it?" He sounded mildly annoyed. "Another dog got hisself run over?" Ben Jay was a sucker for animals and his dad knew it.

Ben Jay was shaking. His face felt all tight. "You better come, there's been a murder."

The sheriff scowled. "Keep your voice down!" he hissed, too late. Everybody in the diner had turned to listen. "Get ahold of yourself and tell me what's going on."

He took a breath. "Lonnie phoned me. He was out near the old place in the woods. Somebody's been"—he dutifully lowered his voice to a whisper—"chopped up in one of the old cabins."

The sheriff looked skeptical. "Anybody we know?" People in the diner laughed.

"Come on, Dad, I'm serious. Lonnie said there's blood all over the place, and . . . body parts."

The sheriff gave him a long look. "You serious, boy? How do you know this isn't one of Lonnie's jokes?"

"Dad, he wouldn't play a trick like this on me. He said to get you and come."

"Why didn't he call me if it's such an emergency?"

Ben Jay was stumped on that one. A flicker of doubt passed through him. *Was* his friend pulling one of his dumb jokes? He quickly put it into perspective. There was no way Lonnie would be crazy enough to include Ben Jay's father in a prank like this. He must've called Ben Jay because he was so upset—automatically punching the number on speed dial. That had to be it.

The sheriff sighed and pushed his plate away. "Save

my puddin'," he called to Linda as he heaved his bulk out of the booth. "One way or the other, I guess we better check it out."

He stuck his hat on his head and they went out to the cruiser parked at the curb. No need to put on the siren and lights. Nobody on the street to get out of the way.

They went down Main Street and made a turn onto Lake Road. At the edge of the water there was a bait and boat rental shop, a fish co-op and the Catfish Bar. The cluster of ramshackle buildings created the kind of quaint atmosphere that brought people to the lake for fishing, but there was little else. Couple of shops in town sold junk disguised as antiques. Down the highway was a motel and some fast-food joints.

The main thing about the lake was the rich people's summer cabins, their docks sticking out into the cola-colored water, their flat-bottom bateaux parked and ready. They had money but didn't spend it in Delonga. Went up to Atlanta instead.

Around the far side of the lake, where the swampy ground seeped toward the lake and the cypress trees stuck out their knees, things were desolate. Muddy logs lurking just below the water could snag a fishing line, rip up a boat. Plenty of water moccasins in there.

To the north were rented cabins, most of them in poor repair now. At one time, when the sheriff's father was alive, it was a popular place for people from Savannah to spend the summer. Back then, Delonga had fancy ice cream parlors, restaurants; there was talk of putting in a golf course. That fell through. Now people went to Florida for Disney, Epcot, places that guaranteed big-time fun. Delonga couldn't compete.

The lake was long and wide in spots, and it took awhile to get around to the site of the alleged murder. Ben Jay sat anxiously in his seat, straining against the seat belt. They saw Lonnie leaning against the fender of his shiny purple truck, smoking.

"He don't look too upset," the sheriff observed aloud. But then he saw the boy's hand was shaking as he brought the cigarette to his lips.

Ben Jay leapt out of the car to join his friend. Lonnie gestured at the cabin and started talking. The sheriff got out more slowly, appraising the scene. As he approached the boys, he noticed his son was turning green around the gills as he listened to what Lonnie had to say.

"Hold on there," the sheriff said. "Start from the beginning and tell it to me. It ain't Ben Jay has to fill out the reports."

Lonnie stopped and attempted to compose himself. "In there. Blood and guts all over. Made me puke." He pointed to a spot in the long grass.

The sheriff passed on inspecting that. "Take your word for it, son. So you're thinking this is a murder scene?" Kid watches too much TV, the sheriff couldn't help thinking.

"Must be," Lonnie said.

"And what makes you so sure?"

"Lots of blood, pieces of . . . body? Looks like someone went crazy in there."

"And you—how do you happen to be here, hanging around a murder scene?"

Lonnie looked scared. "What do you mean? I was out here, I was looking for— I wasn't doing nothing. I . . ."

"Okay, okay hold on. Let me take a look." The sheriff walked up to the cabin door, which was hanging off its hinges. He'd seen dead bodies in his time. Lonnie and Ben Jay could take all the blood and guts they saw in the movies and video games, but a little of the real stuff shook them up pretty bad.

Ben Jay watched his father disappear through the doorway. The woods seemed too quiet. A few whispery rustlings, a far-off bird call. What if the murderer was still around? He looked nervously over his shoulder.

Then he heard his father's voice. "What in hell is this?" He and Lonnie gaped at each other, steeling themselves for bad news. Maybe it was someone they knew? The sheriff came out on the porch. He stood there a moment looking at them, and then he started laughing. Ben Jay thought his father was having a bad reaction, a kind of fit of nervous hysterics. But after a few minutes, he realized his father really was just laughing. Like it was funny. He was laughing so hard he had to bend over and hold his knees.

"You two!" he said when he got control. "A murder?" He waited until Lonnie nodded.

"It's a bunch of damn possums or raccoons. Maybe wild boar. Maybe it's an elk."

"But I didn't see no fur," Lonnie said.

"Gotta call Doc Valentine." The sheriff pulled his phone out of his pocket.

"But he's the vet, Dad," Ben Jay said.

"Right. You got dead animals, you call the vet."

"But if it's murder . . ."

The sheriff looked at Ben Jay patiently. "It's not human. So it's not exactly murder."

Ben Jay thought of the people who had been sent to jail for hurting animals. Beating dogs and letting cats starve to death. Maybe some sicko brought animals here just to torture them. He didn't like the idea. He moved to go up to the cabin to look inside but his dad called him back. He wouldn't let them go near the cabin again until the vet arrived. As they stood around, they gradually began to smell Lonnie's puke. Lonnie lit one cigarette after another. The sheriff glared at the butts on the ground.

"You better give that habit up, boy. You never heard of cancer?"

"Yeah, I know, I'm trying to."

"Trying to get it, you mean?"

Ben Jay snickered, but Lonnie still just looked stunned. When Doc Valentine finally got there, he and the sheriff spent awhile inside the cabin, muttering, coughing and cursing the mess that had started to smell a lot worse than Lonnie's vomit. When the vet came out, he said he agreed with the sheriff but he made it sound more scientific. A large predator had attacked some smaller animals.

"Probably a bear," the doc said, which Ben Jay thought was slightly more reasonable than an elk. There weren't any elks wandering around these Georgia woods, but bears were a possibility, although Ben Jay had never seen one. Anyway, he wasn't convinced. A bear would have needed a huge appetite to eat raccoons, rabbits, skunks like they were stew or something. How could a bear even get so many different animals together at once? It was almost like it'd ordered a take-out meal.

But when he posed the question to Doc Valentine, the man said, "He would have caught them one by one. Might have made the cabin his lair. He just brought his food back to enjoy at his leisure. Nothing strange about it."

So much blood, Ben Jay thought after he sneaked a look inside. Black in places where it had dried, other spots still slick and greasy. He hadn't realized that blood had a smell of its own, like their iron pot when they washed it after boiling beans, or like wood shavings. The mixture of smells started to make him sick. "Okay if we go back?" he asked his dad.

The sheriff looked at the vet. "Think we can let these two investigators go?"

The men laughed. Lonnie looked a little pissed. Ben Jay didn't say good-bye, just got in Lonnie's truck.

Ben Jay couldn't shake what was in his gut. As they drove away, he tore his eyes from his dad and the vet and looked at his friend. "So what do you think?" he asked.

Lonnie stared straight ahead as he drove. "Like your dad says, just animals. I guess it was dumb to get worked up."

Ben Jay was still doubtful. "I just don't know. . . ."

"You don't think that's what it was?"

"I have a weird feeling. Why would a bear toss the buggers around like that? It looked like the kind of thing someone does in a rage, when he's really angry and out of control."

"Maybe that's the way bears feel?" Lonnie gave a weak grin at his joke. "I sure don't know. I just feel stupid."

Ben Jay shook his head. "You did the right thing. What if it had been a murder?"

He couldn't shake the feeling that there was a wrongness in it, something in the cabin that still hung in the air. His father hadn't sensed it at all. Just thought it was funny, critters mashed up like some huge animal pizza. Ben Jay felt sorry for them. He'd feel sorry for anything that ended up dying that way.

"You know," he said, thinking out loud, "after they're finished, why don't we go back up and take another look around?"

"Jeez, I don't know, Ben Jay. . . ."

"You're not scared, are you?" Ben Jay himself *was* a little scared, but he wasn't going to say so.

"I have to admit, I was spooked. Maybe I agree with you, it felt weird. I've seen dead rats and rabbits that some cat caught. My dog swallowed a whole mole once—you should have seen it. He was coughing and I opened his jaws and there was this mole looking out of his throat. But I never saw anything like that mess up in that cabin."

"So we agree? Let's go back. Maybe we'll find something they missed."

"Yeah, like we're CSI guys, right? You heard what your father called us."

Ben Jay didn't think his father had given it enough thought. Made a snap judgment. There he was, complaining that nothing exciting happened in Delonga, and then when it was right in front of his nose, he overlooked it. Blaming that mess on a hungry bear was lame. Ben Jay just didn't believe a bear would stock up that way, almost like taking a trip to the supermarket. He was sure they'd missed something important.

Lonnie interrupted his thoughts. "But if it's not a bear, who or what would do something like that?"

Ben Jay shook his head. "Doc and my father think it's nothing serious because it's just a bunch of dead animals. But they haven't thought about how crazy people always kill animals first. You know, torture cats and dogs before they move on to human victims?"

"You're out there, man," Lonnie said. "You know some strange stuff."

But Ben Jay knew that in the world outside of Delonga, some of that strange stuff was actual fact. He'd done a lot of reading on the subject and he couldn't help wondering: What if there was some sort of serial killer on the loose? Now, *that* was something his father would have to take notice of.

CHAPTER 7

He was watching them from the woods. They didn't know he was there. They couldn't smell him, because he smelled like the woods, like the earth, like the animals. He knew how to be quiet, how to make himself go still, barely breathing. That was the way to hunt, like his daddy said.

But he'd made a mistake. When he'd found the cabin, no one had been around. It looked deserted, like a good place to hide, low down and dark. It was in the dark that he hunted and captured his prey, then slept by day. He had been sleeping when the sound of the motor startled him awake. He knew the sound meant trouble. Didn't stop to see, just went out the broken window at the back. He was fast, gone into the woods before the truck arrived.

Now people were there, looking at his hiding place.

Not a good idea to attract the interest of people. Once people came around, started snooping, they wouldn't stop until they made things bad for you. He would have to move, find another place. He was tired. He would like to lie down and close his eyes.

After a long time of waiting, they went away in their vehicles. The woods were quiet for a while, as if making sure the people were really gone. Then they came back to life, rustling, shaking, chirping, screeching. Cautiously, he crawled out of his hiding place. He could smell the men, their human smell. They left their footprints in the blood, tracking out into the dust.

He sat down and thought. What to do and where to go? When he first ran out of the burning house, he thought he would run until he got to . . . something. Something that would be waiting for him. Something with the answers. So far, no answers had appeared. Now it was only more running. It made him tired.

He squatted down on the floor of the cabin, closed his eyes but didn't go to asleep. He had to think, even if he didn't want to. Think about the house and the room and the night travels, and the screams. Think about whether he had done the right thing.

A mess in his mind. Hard to know what was right or wrong. Daddy says one thing, Mama says another. Deep down in his mind he always knew that what they did was bad. Couldn't say it to Daddy. Had to behave. Now he wanted it out of his head, wanted to throw it away, never think of it again.

But thoughts keep coming back. Pictures in his head, like a TV show. Everything jumbled up in one big mess. A feeling kept pushing at his brain. Didn't want to think about it. But it came out anyway. Truth was, he missed it. He looked around the cabin at the blood and carcasses and it just wasn't the same. Not as good as it was back there. He missed the feel of them. Missed the screaming. Missed the taste of human blood.

CHAPTER 8

They finally had to stop for gas.

"What about supplies?" Gena asked. "Aren't we going to need things like food and toilet paper?"

Naturally she hadn't been able to bring anything like food with her. Her mother would have been suspicious. She had packed clothes, a toothbrush, soap, shampoo. Being too practical for her own good, she worried not only about what they were going to eat but also about things like toilet paper.

"Yeah, and don't forget the bread," Maryann said. "Did you ever notice that whenever there's a hurricane warning, everybody runs out to buy toilet paper and bread? What's the connection?"

"I was just thinking, that's all," Gena replied quietly.

"Yeah, we seriously don't want to wipe our butts on newspaper!"

"Don't be such a smartass, Maryann," Casey said. "Gena's right. We need to stop somewhere and pick up a few things. There's a market in Delonga, but it's probably not a good idea to go there. I seem to remember there's a supercenter off the highway about ten miles before we get to town."

"Are people gonna recognize you?" Gena asked nervously. "Call your parents?"

"Nobody will even see us," Casey replied confidently. "We just drive right through town and up to the lake. Nobody will know we're there."

Gena felt better when they were actually inside the supermarket, pushing carts around and grabbing stuff off the shelves. Frozen mac and cheese, frozen pizza and lasagna, strawberry cheesecake and toaster pastries. They went crazy and bought only junk food. It was a vacation, they told themselves.

"So, should we get toilet paper?" Gena couldn't help asking, and they all cracked up. Casey and Maryann told her to get the supersize pack.

It was early afternoon when they finally got to Delonga. Gena now knew why Casey called it stone country. It wasn't much of a town, just a long main street and some shady lanes going off on the sides. Two storefronts had striped awnings and big pots with flowers out front, but most of the street looked ordinary and shabby. A diner on the corner had a sign that winked on and off in pink neon: LINDA'S DINER. Looking at it, Gena realized she was hungry.

Just as Casey had predicted, no one paid much attention to the car. She didn't stop, just drove through and turned onto Lake Road. It was a paved road for a while and then it abruptly turned into dirt. The limbs of the huge live oaks on either side reached out and joined, turning the road into a long green tunnel. Gena wondered if they would be roughing it in the cabin. Everything looked so wild and lonely.

When they arrived, Gena realized how far from reality her imagination had been. The cabin was bigger than she had thought it would be. They got out and she took a deep breath. The air was fresh and piney with just a little undertone of dampness. Inside, the cabin was hardly rustic. There was no question of having to rough it. She should have known, it being Casey's family's place. There was a big living room with a stone fireplace. Carpet on the floor. The kitchen had Formica counters and stainless steel fixtures. There was a fridge, a microwave, even a dishwasher. Two bedrooms and a modern bathroom were on the second floor. The place smelled musty, but they opened the windows to air it out.

"Let's eat something," Maryann said, pulling a jar of peanut butter from their paper sacks and opening a loaf of bread. Gena poured glasses of milk and they sat around the dinette table stuffing their faces.

"Oh shit!" Gena suddenly remembered something. "I was supposed to call my mother when I got to Washington. Do you think we'd be there by now?"

Casey shook her head. "It's a ten-hour trip at least,

maybe more if they make stops. You have plenty of time. What we need to do now is take a walk."

Maryann groaned. "I need a nap."

"Come on," Casey insisted. "We've been sitting in the car for hours. We'll work up an appetite and grill hamburgers outside for dinner. Get your butts in gear, ladies."

Casey could have cared less about building up an appetite. What she really wanted to do was see if Lane and his friends were out on the lake. From what Lane had said, she knew the boys' cabin was on the far side, where the small rental places were. If they didn't run into him now, she'd suggest a boat ride tomorrow. They'd go across the lake in the bateau and just happen to land at Lane's doorstep.

She could hardly wait to see his face when she surprised him.

CHAPTER 9

Ben Jay and Lonnie decided to get pizza. They sat outside in the truck, eating and talking about the massacre. That was Ben Jay's name for it now.

The one thing that bothered Ben Jay was why Lonnie had been there in the woods. He had asked him, trying to sound casual. Not that he believed Lonnie had anything to do with killing animals, and not that he didn't have the right to be there in the woods. But what a coincidence to be on the spot in the middle of the day, when he should've been doing his job at Becker's service station. Right away, he could tell that Lonnie was uncomfortable with the question.

"I was around, you know?" Lonnie looked away, changed the subject. "Hey, I think I found a good spot to get some squirrels."

"Yeah. Like squirrels are hard to get," Ben Jay

remarked. You wanted to shoot squirrels, all you had to do was walk out your back door. "You took off work today?"

"Told me not to come in. They got some new dude, he can do things, a real mechanic. Becker doesn't need me. I'm gonna be broke-ass again."

Ben Jay took a minute. "So you went up to the lake." A statement. He wasn't interrogating, not acting like his father.

Lonnie just shrugged, took another bite of pizza.

Ben Jay waited a couple of beats. "You gonna tell me? Or you keeping it a deep dark secret?" They'd been friends a long time, since they were practically babies. What was the big deal? "Come on, man, you keep this up I'm gonna think you developed a taste for skunk."

"Okay, okay." Lonnie laughed self-consciously. "Truth is . . ." A hesitation. "I was looking for Norleen."

It took a minute to hit Ben Jay. Norleen?

"I know what you're thinking."

"I'm not thinking anything right now. My mind is a complete blank. What would Norleen be doing up in the woods and why were you chasing her?"

"I wasn't *chasing* her!" Lonnie retorted. "I seen Pope's car go up there. Norleen was with him. You know he's bad news."

Ben Jay thought about it. "So was she being abducted or something?" he joked.

"She was with him, that's enough. She's gonna get herself into trouble hanging with him."

"Maybe she likes him."

"Nobody likes Pope."

"Come on, Lonnie. You have no cause to be prying into Norleen's business."

"If she's with Pope, it's my business."

Then it dawned on him and he started laughing. "You're sweet on her! Lonnie's in *love!*"

He watched in awe as a bright red blush crept up from Lonnie's neck and spread over his normally pinkish face. The skin slowly turned almost purple.

"Jeez, don't have a heart attack on me!"

"Just drop it, okay?" Lonnie looked a little pissed.

"Sure, sure, okay. It's your business." But Ben Jay couldn't stop smiling. He'd never thought Lonnie would be interested in a girl like Norleen. Norleen had purple streaks in her hair, a tattoo on her neck, metal in her eyebrows, and a ring in her navel for all the world to see in the space between her cropped tops and tight jeans. She was one of a kind in a place like Delonga. Some of the kids got pierced, even had tattoos, but nothing like Norleen. He would have thought Lonnie was too shy to even look at her.

"I think Norleen can take care of herself," Ben Jay said.

"She gets herself into a lot of bad situations," Lonnie persisted.

"How would you know? You been following her around? You better watch out, my dad will take you in for stalking." Ben Jay was half kidding, half serious. If

Lonnie was following Norleen, and Norleen was hanging out with Pope, Lonnie could get himself into more trouble than the Sheriff taking him in. At least more serious in terms of pain—he could get himself into a fight. Then suddenly Ben Jay had a thought. "Wait a minute! Were they at the cabin? Was Pope there?"

Lonnie looked at him. "You think Pope would do something like that?"

"Far as I'm concerned, Pope and nasty go together," Ben Jay replied.

"But kill all those animals and rip them apart? Nah, I don't think so. Anyway, he was with Norleen. She wouldn't get mixed up with that."

As if Lonnie knew what Norleen got mixed up with, Ben Jay thought, even though he basically agreed. Pope's preference was for tearing up people, not animals.

"Well, what do you say we take a ride up there?" Ben Jay asked again.

"What—now?" Lonnie looked at the sky with a worried expression, like he expected a tornado. "It's getting late. It'll be too dark to see. Let's wait till tomorrow."

"Tomorrow they'll be cleaning things up. If we want to find anything, we have to go today."

Lonnie hesitated. "I don't know."

"You scared?"

"No, I'm not scared."

"Maybe we'll bump into Norleen and Pope," Ben Jay teased. "Anyway, did you see them at all this morning?"

Lonnie shook his head dejectedly. "Never caught up

with them—don't know where they went. She shouldn't be hanging around him."

"You said. But you ever think maybe Norleen is just Pope's type? They kind of match."

Lonnie puffed up. "They don't. Norleen just doesn't know what she's doing."

Ben Jay sighed. There was no talking to him. Lonnie would have to find out for himself.

"Fine," he said, letting Lonnie have his way. "But let's go up there and take a look before dark."

"I don't know, man."

"We see anything we don't like, we leave right away, okay? This bear, or whatever it is, doesn't have wheels, does he? We can take off."

Lonnie was not enthusiastic but he agreed to go with Ben Jay, thinking maybe he'd still catch a glimpse of Norleen and Pope together. He figured if he was with the sheriff's son, Pope wouldn't dare try anything.

The boys wiped their hands and mouths and dumped their greasy napkins in the trash barrel. They climbed into the truck and drove down through town and onto Lake Road. Lonnie fumbled for his pack of cigarettes. He really wanted to quit, but he couldn't do it when he was feeling nervous like this.

"What made you go to that place? Why'd you look inside?" Ben Jay asked, still slightly troubled by Lonnie's presence at the cabin.

Lonnie looked startled, as if he had forgotten something and just remembered it. "You know . . . I think I saw *it*. I mean, that's why I stopped, I was passing the cabin and I saw something moving inside. I thought it was Norleen and Pope. So I pulled up and I was going to take a look."

"Thinking to catch them in the act?" That was all Pope would need to get riled up.

"Aw, man. I was just worried, you know? I wanted to make sure she was okay."

"Lonnie," Ben Jay said patiently. "Let me explain something to you. Norleen was with Pope because she wanted to be with him. She didn't need rescuing."

Lonnie wasn't buying it. "How would you know? Anyway, it turned out it wasn't them, was it? But I didn't know that when I looked inside. I saw all the blood, I figured Pope killed her."

Ben Jay wanted to laugh but managed to hold it in. He could tell his friend was embarrassed. "I can believe it," he said as seriously as he could. "But before that, you said you saw movement. You stopped. Did you hear anything?"

Lonnie took a long pull at the cigarette and flipped the butt out the window. "Yeah. Scratching, scrabbling, like a cat trying to get out of a box."

"Like someone, or something, was hauling ass?"

"Yeah. I figured it was Pope. I was really shook. All I could think of was to call for help. That's when I called you."

They had to pull off the lake road and onto a dirt track to reach the cabin. Ben Jay realized that Lonnie couldn't have just been passing by the cabin like he said. He must have purposely driven up the rutted track. But why? Had he followed Pope and Norleen out there before? Lonnie could get himself in serious trouble, and not just with Pope. Norleen was the type who would take things into her own hands.

But this was no time for warning Lonnie about it. They'd reached the cabin and it was staring at them, broken windows like blackened eyes.

"Let's do it," Ben Jay said, and got out of the truck, but Lonnie stayed put, lighting another cigarette.

The smell of dead flesh was getting worse. That morning it hadn't been as bad. Which meant the mess hadn't been there all that long if it was just starting to rot. Either this was a one-gulp bear or something entirely different had been going on. Ben Jay forced himself to step up to the doorway and look in. The place was empty, except for the mess, of course. Which made him gag almost immediately. Before turning away he noticed a window at the back, broken out like the rest of them. A possible escape route. Maybe that's what Lonnie had heard, someone going out the window. He turned back to the truck. "You coming or what?"

"Aw, man." Lonnie opened the door and got out, eyeing the cabin with apprehension.

"Nothing in there you haven't seen before. Let's take a look around the side."

Lonnie followed Ben Jay, muttering about the smell and the briars as they turned the corner to the back of the cabin. Brambles and vines had grown up right to the cabin walls, some of them curling into the broken window. But there were fresh breaks in the branches, and the leaves were crushed. Ben Jay stopped. "Look at this here. Somebody came out the window, all right. That's what you heard."

They could see a rough path where the animal, or whatever it was, had pushed through the undergrowth. "You're not planning on going in them woods, are you?" Lonnie asked.

Ben Jay was tempted to see if he could find a trail, but it was beginning to get dark. There were rustling sounds of nocturnal animals waking up. A screech owl gave its mournful wail in the trees. Ben Jay thought his dad should have investigated further than he did, should have made it his business to poke around instead of blaming that mess on a bear.

He was about to turn away when the last horizontal rays of the setting sun caught a glint of metal at his feet. He reached down, felt around in the leaves and pulled out an object. A long old-fashioned key with a curlicue at the end. The kind of key he had seen in his aunt Lottie's antebellum house in Macon; a skeleton key that fit all the bedroom doors. He couldn't imagine a key like this being used in a cabin in Delonga.

"Come on," Lonnie called, already headed back to the truck. By the time Ben Jay caught up, Lonnie was inside with the engine running. He had the truck moving before Ben Jay could shut his door.

"Place gives me the creeps," Lonnie said, tearing back down the road.

"Take it easy, man."

Lonnie skidded around a curve. "That was a big waste of time. We didn't find nothing."

Ben Jay held up the key.

Lonnie looked at it, blank. "Some old key, what?"

"Found it near that broken window. Shouldn't have been there."

"Who says? What's so important about some old key been lying there for a coon's age?"

"Doesn't fit the picture. It's a key like they used in big ol' fancy houses. There's no fancy houses in these woods. Just the cabins."

Lonnie was quiet for a while and then he said, "You're wrong."

"Huh?"

"You're wrong about the old houses. You forgot the plantation. Damn!" He hit the steering wheel with his fist. "I should've looked up there. That's where Pope would go, not in one of those chickenshit cabins."

The plantation. Built in the eighteen hundreds. It was abandoned now. Part of it had been burned by Sherman on his march to the sea. Just the kind of place for a key like that. The plantation was pretty far away from the cabin, but hell, the stupid key *could* have come from there. Kids were always fooling around the old place—for the most part it had been picked clean. The key probably had no connection at all to the massacre.

Ben Jay felt deflated. Here he thought he'd found a clue. What a jerk.

"Hey, man, you look like you're gonna cry," Lonnie said. He was in a better mood now that he'd put some distance between him and the cabin.

"It's nothing."

"You still think your dad is wrong?"

"It wasn't a bear."

Lonnie sighed. "I kind of agree. We've been camping and hunting in those woods how long? Never saw hide nor hair of a bear. A bear would have been after our food, if nothing else. If there really is a bear, it's a new one, that's for sure."

Ben Jay smiled. That was Lonnie. You thought he had nothing in his head but air and then he came up with sense.

Lonnie dropped Ben Jay off at the end of his road, anxious to get home. Or maybe he was still anxious to find out where Norleen was at.

"You be good, Lonnie," Ben Jay said as he got out.

"I'm good."

Ben Jay watched the truck go off. He walked up to the house, which was still dark, his father not home yet. He had been home alone countless nights, but for the first time he gave in to the urge to turn on all the lights and search the rooms, even looking under his bed. Nothing there, of course. He grabbed a soda from the kitchen, went back to his bedroom and put the key in his desk drawer. Then he fired up the computer. He still had some things to find out. Specifically about animals and how they ate. Particularly animals with bad tempers and big appetites.

Whether or not the key had anything to do with it didn't matter. There were lots of questions that had to be answered, and if his father wasn't interested, it was up to him.

CHAPTER 10

In the woods, dark came down fast. The air was cooler, and touched with moisture from the lake. The girls were making their way back to the cabin, pushing through the undergrowth. At first they had been following a rough trail, but then gradually they had strayed off the path. Casey was leading; none of them were saying much. They were hot and sticky from the humidity, and tired. Maybe a little nervous as darkness closed in. They all jumped when a tremulous scream rang through the trees.

"What was that?" Maryann asked.

"A screech owl," Casey said calmly, although she had been startled herself.

"Hope he's not gonna keep that up all night," Maryann said with an uncomfortable giggle. She looked around. "Hey, is this the way we came? It doesn't look familiar."

"Omigod, are we lost?" Gena exclaimed, and then immediately bit her tongue.

"Calm down, guys," Casey said, starting to sound exasperated. Gena couldn't blame her. "I know the way back. It's not like we're in the jungle."

Might as well be, Gena thought. She hoped Casey really knew where she was going. These woods weren't like the ones up north where she came from. They were completely foreign, with spooky-looking moss hanging off the trees, and some really horrible-smelling plants. And what about snakes? Should they be walking around in here like this? Gena decided not to say anything—Casey and Maryann already thought she was a worrywart. But there was also the other thing: she could swear she heard something walking behind them. Better not say anything about that either, she decided. They'd think she was crazy. Probably an animal, she told herself, wondering how big the animals in these woods might be.

Now that the sun was down, all kinds of bugs started biting. Gena smacked at them in silence, relieved when Maryann started bitching about them too.

"If I'd known you two were such babies—" Casey started.

But Maryann interupted. "Hey! What's that?"

Casey gave a dramatic sigh. "What's what?"

"That noise," Maryann snapped, but her voice was a hoarse whisper. "Like somebody walking in there." She pointed at the thick patch of dark trees.

Casey stopped and put her hands on her hips. She

hadn't heard any noise, but if there actually *was* something out here, she hoped it was Lane and his friends. Had Lane believed her after all? He could have found out where her family's cabin was. A chill of excitement went up her spine. She forced herself not to look around, to act casual in case it was him and he was watching her. She certainly didn't want to look like a scared little girl. "Like, we're in the woods, you know? And things live in the woods. Ever heard of rabbits, squirrels, possums?"

"Snakes," Gena couldn't help saying, but Casey ignored her.

"Animals make noise. How scary is that?"

"Depends on the size of the animals," Maryann answered.

"Well, maybe it's Bigfoot." Casey laughed, raising her voice a little, hoping Lane might hear.

Maryann copied Casey's stance, hands on hips. "I'm not afraid of *him,*" she said. "But the deer flies are doing a good job of eating me alive. How about it, Case? Are we almost back to the cabin?"

Casey gave an impatient snort and tossed her head. "There's some Deet at the house. Y'all better be sure to spray yourselves next time."

As they rounded a sharp bend, the cabin appeared—tucked away in the dense woods. Maryann and Gena cheered, but Casey dragged her feet, still hoping Lane would materialize. She *had* heard something, finally, scuffing through the leaves and brush. She stopped to listen again. Nothing except the normal sounds of the woods.

Everyone was hungry, but as soon as they walked through the front door they all collapsed in the living room—they were so beat that nobody made a move to start cooking.

"Too bad this hotel doesn't have room service," Maryann said with a moan.

"I wish," Gena sighed. "I'm too tired to think about even defrosting a pizza. Hey, could we drive into town? What about that place Linda's?"

"Well, we could," Casey replied smugly. "But we're not supposed to be here, remember? We're in Washington, D.C."

Gena screeched and jumped off the couch. "My mother! I have to call her!"

"No sweat, Gena," Casey said, trying to calm her down. "We'd only be arriving about now. We have to check in, find our rooms, unpack. You wouldn't be on the phone the minute you got there, would you?"

"Sorry. I'm just a little nervous."

Casey rolled her eyes and grinned. "A little?"

Gena told herself again to cool it. Why couldn't she relax?

"I just about have the strength to unscrew the top of one of those jugs of wine," Casey said, getting up from the couch.

Gena was about to say she didn't want any wine, but maybe it would help her relax. Alcohol was a big issue with her mother—but hey, what she didn't know wouldn't kill her.

"I'll get it," Maryann said, suddenly energetic. "And I'll start a fire. We're having burgers, right?"

"Sounds good to me," Casey said.

"Me too," Gena agreed brightly. Should she offer to help? Or would that be another wrong move? Casey seemed good with just letting Maryann take over. Maybe she should act the same. She hated feeling so uncertain. She wished her mind would just calm down and shut up.

Maryann brought in the gallon jugs of chardonnay and three wineglasses from the kitchen. "Unfortunately, it's warm, and those old ice cubes in the freezer taste terrible."

Casey sighed. "Who cares, just bring it on."

When they were served, Casey raised her glass. "A toast. To us . . . having a great time on the class trip!" Privately, she was toasting to having a great time with Lane.

"I second that," Maryann said.

"Me too," Gena added. She took a sip of the wine. It had a sour taste. But what did she know, maybe chardonnay was supposed to taste like that.

Gradually, they all relaxed, the wine putting them in a good mood. Maryann went out and tended the fire, and Gena finally decided she would help. They made hamburger patties, and soon the delicious aroma of grilling meat was wafting through the air. Suddenly, Gena realized she was actually having fun. Somewhere between the first sip of wine and this last one, she had become calm. She would deal with her mother later. After all, she had just arrived in D.C. Her mother would just have to wait.

CHAPTER 11

Trash followed the red car all the way to a shitty little town called Delonga. There was a moment on the main street when he was sure the girls spotted him. He hung back and watched them make a right near a bait shop. The sign at the turn said LAKE ROAD. Not exactly what you'd call a highway. There was no other traffic, so he had to hang way back. When the surface changed to dirt, he stayed back even more, hoping there were no turnoffs. He let the car get ahead and then lost sight of it. After about five minutes of bumpy road he pulled up to a fork and had to make a choice. Too bad there were none of those convenient clues you saw in movies— telltale clouds of dust kicked up by the car you were chasing. He had to pick, and he picked wrong because he never did catch sight of the red car again. He made a tight turn on the narrow road, came to another fork and realized he didn't have a clue where he was or where he was going.

By the time he'd gone up and down the rutted roads, getting nowhere, he was fixing to get one bitch of a headache. When the girls had stopped at the supermarket, he'd grabbed a couple of candy bars, a bag of chips and a soda. Now he was coming down from a sugar high, not to mention the hangover still lurking behind his eyes. The sorry state of the road wasn't helping either. The truck shook as it went over the ruts, making his brain rattle in his head. He had to find a place to stop and close his eyes for a minute. He felt like just pulling onto the side of the road, but he'd probably fall asleep, and it wasn't worth the chance of getting hit by a car coming around the bend.

There was a track up ahead—dirt that had once been layered with gravel. He turned in, bumped and bounced over even worse ruts. He came to a run-down cabin with a few rusted metal chairs out front, empty plastic trash bins lying on their sides, lots of junk on the porch. The place looked deserted. He turned off the engine, moved the seat back so he could stretch his legs. He had to grab some z's for a couple of minutes. He leaned back and shut his eyes. His head throbbed; even his teeth ached. He was just dozing off when he started getting eaten alive. Fricking sand gnats! He rolled up the windows to keep them out, but that lasted only a minute before he started to sweat. The heat made him feel like he might puke. He opened the door and slid out, stood looking around, slapping flies. The best thing to do was to get inside the cabin.

The door was locked, but with a quick kick and shove, it popped open. Inside was hot as hell, but there were no bugs. He pushed up a couple of windows, relieved to see they had screens, and took a dive onto an old brown and yellow plaid couch. Made it just before he thought he would puke for sure. Lying flat, he felt better. He'd just take a quick nap, then go back home. Following those chicks was one of the stupidest ideas he'd ever had. What did he think he was going to accomplish? Asshole.

He closed his eyes and took a deep breath. The slightest of breezes stirred at the windows and he felt himself sinking down deep. Dreaming of the sound of footsteps on gravel. He came half awake and thought of his truck—had he locked it up? But he had the keys, right? A scuffling near the front door. He'd shut it, right? He'd put an old wooden chair against it, since he'd broken the lock getting in. He meant to get up to check but somehow he didn't get around to it. Nobody around here anyway. Started dreaming about some old hound his daddy used to own. They went hunting—he could hear the crack of the rifle in his ears. And while he slept, darkness fell.

CHAPTER 12

Ben Jay was surfing the Web. Lots of animals, even insects, gathered and stored food. Squirrels won the prize for being the biggest hogs, stockpiling more than they could ever use. As far as he could tell, the only animals that seemed big enough to do something like what they'd seen in the cabin were bears and bobcats, natural-born killers. Bears attacked cows and chickens around these parts in the old days, but they'd all been killed off by farmers. He knew bears had made a comeback in Georgia, but, as Lonnie had said, in all this time they had never actually *seen* a bear in this vicinity. Never heard of anyone else in Delonga seeing one either. Bobcats were mostly down near the Okefenokee swamp and Folkston. They ate mice, shrews, rabbits, wild fowl—any kind of animal, really. But a bobcat wasn't very big. Ben Jay couldn't see a bobcat bringing a bunch of animals into a cabin for a banquet. So a bear really was more likely.

What he read was all very interesting but didn't tell him spit. He was sure he was dealing with something else entirely. Something that could not be explained by ordinary facts. He had a strange feeling that what had happened up at that cabin was not at all normal—which led him to look for some not-very-normal Web sites.

FARMERS DISCOVER MUTILATED CATTLE.

That was more like it. Mutilated was the word that described the animals he'd seen. That was one of the things that had been so strange. Instead of being consumed, the carcasses had been torn apart and thrown around. It was totally brutal. He paged down and read:

On February 15, 1998, Greg Hickson, a cattle breeder in La Pointe, Alabama, went out to his pasture in the early hours of the morning and found a calf from his herd lying on its side. It looked unhurt, but close inspection revealed that a circle of skin was missing near its navel. All the blood had been drained from the body, though there was no sign of blood in the surrounding earth. Larry Warren, at Peachtree Farm in Georgia, was greeted by an equally perplexing scene when he discovered that one of his cows had been mutilated. Its ears, tongue, right eye, and udders had been removed. The cow had also been drained of blood. In both cases, there were no signs of struggle or of a predatory animal attack. Warren reported to local law officials that he had seen coyotes in the area that morning, but they had avoided the dead animal—strange behavior for these scavengers. "In any case," Warren said, "coyotes attack at the neck and then eat the animal. There were no bite marks on the cow."

Similar events have been reported in other states for many years. Corpses are found bloodless but with no sign of blood at the scene. The mutilated parts of the animal are cut off neatly, "as if with a scalpel," one rancher observed. Most disturbing of all is the fact that none of the missing organs have ever been recovered.

Police have called the attacks ritualistic. Some locals have blamed farmers for the incidents. "I been in this business forty years and I've never seen nothing like this," Warren said. "I'm too old to be playing jokes."

Other locals claim the mutilations are the work of aliens; still others blame it on the chupacabra or goatsucker, a creature that supposedly kills livestock and drains the animals' blood. Although the legend originated primarily in the Caribbean, Mexico, and Central America, there are stories of the goatsucker closer to home, in the state of Florida.

Ben Jay stopped at a link to a site for the goatsucker myth and clicked on it. A list of books about bloodsucking animals started running down his computer screen. It looked like there could be hundreds. There were a lot of legends about the chupacabra. Another myth was the loup-garou, but Ben Jay quickly realized that was simply a werewolf. Then, of course, there were the vampires, the most famous bloodsuckers of all.

He was about to turn back to the more factual site when he saw a link to a newspaper in Georgia that was reporting on similar stuff. A recent headline immediately caught his eye: HAS ANYONE SEEN THIS CREATURE? MONSTER STALKS GREAT SMOKY MOUNTAINS AND BEYOND, *by Megan McCauley.*

Ben Jay read only the first few paragraphs before deciding to print it all out. He read the article slowly, then read the whole thing over again. There were uncanny similarities with what he had seen in the cabin. A virtual swath of animal massacres stretched from Tennessee to Georgia. And if he had his specs right, they were heading toward Delonga. For a moment he thought it must all be a joke. But would someone really go to the trouble of posting a phony story about some monster, then creating a bloody scene to show that it had arrived? Seemed like a lot trouble for something that would only be discovered by chance. Again, the uneasiness about Lonnie's presence at the cabin nagged at the back of his mind. He brushed it away. Pope was more likely to pull a hoax involving dead animals. Could it have been Pope luring Lonnie to discover it? Ben Jay shook his head clear. All too elaborate, and Lonnie couldn't have pretended innocence that well. Still, Ben Jay would feel like a jerk if he had been taken in.

He read the report again. This couldn't be a joke,

and certainly not one of Pope's making. The newspaper was real, and he could check on the reporter. He was thinking about actually phoning the newspaper to see if he could talk to the reporter when he heard his father come in.

"Ben Jay, you here?"

"Hey, Dad," he said absently, still intent on the pages on his desk.

The sheriff came to the bedroom door. "Sorry I'm so late. You eat?"

"Lonnie and me got pizza."

"Good." The sheriff sighed. He sounded tired. "I tell you, son, it never rains but it pours."

"Something else happen?" Ben Jay asked, alert. Another massacre?

"More animal trouble. Some people up at the lake reported their dog is gone. Think its been stolen. Who would be stealing a dog around here?"

"Maybe it was in that cabin, with the other . . . things," Ben Jay said.

"Nope. Went missing this evening, little poodle thing no bigger than a popcorn fart. Some kind of show dog, that's why they're so upset. You ever heard of show dog thieves? Who would even think there'd be some show dog around here?"

"Maybe it just ran away?"

"It would, if it knew what was good for it. That woman made me want to run away myself."

Ben Jay had a soft heart for animals, especially dogs.

He didn't like thinking about an animal that wasn't used to the outdoors being lost in the woods. He didn't like to think what might happen, considering. "You going out to look for it?"

His father snorted. "What, call out a posse? It'll be back when it's hungry." He reflected a moment. "Name is Biscuit. What kind of name is that?" He sighed. "I'm going to sit on my ass. I'm wore out from all this excitement."

His father left the room and Ben Jay could hear him settling into his recliner in the living room. Ben Jay decided to he'd call the newspaper and ask to speak to this Megan McCauley. He'd do it before he lost his nerve. But suddenly his father was back at the bedroom door.

"Another thing," he said. "What's up with your pal Lonnie?"

"I don't know, what?"

"I see his truck heading onto Lake Road with that big light of his on the side turned on. Then he sees the cruiser and he does a one-eighty, turns off the light and heads out toward home. Mighty suspicious behavior, don't you think? What's he up to?"

What the heck was going on? Was Lonnie chasing Pope again?

"Lonnie was shook up, you know?" he said to his father. "Maybe he thought he'd go check out the woods for bears."

His dad gave him a look and shook his head. "You

tell Lonnie I want to have a word with him. I don't need a loose cannon in the woods with a searchlight. I'll be the one taking care of things."

"I don't think it was a bear, Dad."

"Well then, maybe it was E.T." His father winked and went off laughing to himself.

It took Ben Jay a second to get it. E.T., the extra-terrestrial from that old movie. He didn't think they had to worry about dealing with aliens. But his father didn't know how close they were to the possibility that something strange was going on out there in the woods.

Chapter 13

"Gena, are you feeling okay?" her mother asked. Gena had to stifle giggles. Course she was feeling okay. She was feeling terrific.

"Yes, Mom, I'm fine. Look, I gotta go. The kids are calling me."

"Okay, dear, have fun. Don't forget to call tomorrow, now."

"Yes, Mom." Gena hit End on Casey's cell phone and the stifled laughter came spurting out. "God, that was close. Did I sound sober? I didn't slur my words, did I?"

Casey gave her a look. "Gena, you only had one glass of wine. That's hardly enough to get cooked."

But one glass had been enough to make her head feel like it was stuffed with cotton and to give her an amazing floating feeling. Everything seemed better and funnier.

And now that the phone call was out of the way, she felt really free.

Maryann shouted from the kitchen that the burgers were ready. She had brought them in from the grill, along with the smell of charcoal fire and evening air.

They sat in the kitchen, the table covered with bottles of ketchup, mustard, hot sauce, pickles, bags of potato chips, cans of soda and the jug of wine.

"We should have bought graham crackers, marshmallows and some chocolate bars," Gena said. "We could make s'mores."

"Yum! Maybe we can get some tomorrow," Maryann said. "What do you think, Casey?"

"Mmmm?" Casey's mind was as far away from s'mores as it could get. All she could think about doing tomorrow was seeing Lane—she wouldn't have time to go shopping. On the other hand, it *did* sound like something they could do with the guys, build a campfire out in the woods and roast marshmallows. Sit together by the firelight. They'd have to drive out of Delonga to get the stuff, though. No sense letting herself be seen by someone who knew her parents. *Oh, by the way, wasn't that Casey I saw up here in April?*

"Earth to Casey," Maryann said when she got no answer. "I cooked. You clean."

Gena saw Casey's face and jumped in. "I'll do it. It's paper plates anyway."

"Well, you still have to wash them, you know,"

Maryann said. "And then put them out by the grill to dry."

Gena looked at her.

Maryann kept a straight face for a moment; then she and Casey started laughing.

Gena felt her face burn but she laughed along with them. "Right, we always wash ours at home, too." It was lame. Why did she feel like she was always the butt of their jokes?

The two of them went back to the living room carrying the wine jug and she heard them doing something with the fireplace. Gena gathered up all the plates and paper cups and shoved them into a plastic trash bag. Then she washed the cutlery and cleaned off the table. What about the grill? She looked out the door. The coals were still glowing under a layer of white ash. Too bad, perfect for s'mores. She stepped outside with the trash bag and the screen door slapped shut behind her. The night was almost pitch-black. She looked up and was stunned. A million stars glittered overhead. It was an entirely different sky than the one she'd left back in the city.

She stood there, stirring the coals with a stick, watching the sparks, just letting her mind drift, glad that the guilts had subsided for a while. They'd probably come back tomorrow when she had to phone her mom again. But for now, it was peaceful.

When she happened to glance up, the woods suddenly seemed to have moved closer, like they'd been sneaking up on her when she wasn't looking and had stopped just before she could catch them at it. In an instant the peacefulness she was enjoying left her and a chill went down her spine. Things could be in there between the trees, watching her. She dropped the stick and ran back into the lighted house.

"Come on in here, Gena," Casey called, hearing the door slam. "We're gonna tell ghost stories."

"There's a prize for the best one," Maryann added.

Gena collected herself and walked into the room, trying to act casual. "And what would that be?" she asked. She wasn't really in the mood for ghosts.

Casey got a sly look on her face. "You have to wait to find out."

They were at it again, two against one. But she sat down on the floor next to the fireplace and tried to force that peaceful mood back into her mind. It'll be just like summer camp, she told herself.

"Wait—are the doors locked?" Maryann asked, looking over her shoulder.

Gena couldn't tell if she was serious. "I locked the kitchen door when I came back in." Then she felt like an idiot—they would think she was acting like a twelve-year-old again. She decided she'd better tell a story to prove she wasn't the wuss they thought she was.

"Okay. I'll go first." She lowered her voice, tried to sound dramatic. "There was a woman in my neighborhood who invited her entire family for Thanksgiving dinner. They were impressed because she wasn't much of a cook. When they arrived, they found the table set with the best china and crystal. Fabulous aromas were coming out of the kitchen. They could hear the crackle of meat roasting. The woman had obviously outdone herself. They could hardly wait to eat. Finally, they were seated at the table, and she comes out with a big tray with a silver cover on top. Everybody's mouth is watering for the turkey. She puts down the tray and lifts the cover. *Ta-da!* It's not a turkey after all. . . . It's . . . a . . . roast baby!"

"Gee, that was original," Maryann said, yawning.

"Come on, Gena. That's from the fourth grade," Casey said. "There's no way anyone would believe that one anymore."

"Ghost stories aren't supposed to be *true*," Gena said.

"Yes, but if they're true, they're scarier," Casey insisted. "I propose some rules. You can only tell stories that scare *you* and only stories you can verify are true."

"Okay, okay. Here's one I *know* is true. My cousin's girlfriend's sister went to Mexico and got a bite on her face. She figured it was a mosquito but the bite got swollen and grew bigger and bigger. When she got home she went to the doctor and got a shot but it didn't work. So one morning she decides to pop it, 'cause it's like a big zit— but when she popped it, out come all these black spiders!"

"Total rule breaker! That was in a movie I saw," Casey said.

The last of Gena's good mood was evaporating. "Okay, then you tell one."

"Okay. I will."

Casey grabbed the wine jug, poured herself another glass and took a deep breath. "This one really is true," she said dramatically. "My aunt actually saw it; she was there. It happened when she was in high school. There was a girl in her class who was really unpopular. Her hair was a disaster, she had bad skin, a real mess. But she kept talking about how she had this great date for the prom. Everybody was like, *no way*. But she kept telling them about her dress and getting a corsage, and finally they felt sorry for her and what were clearly delusions.

"But on the night of the prom, after the dance started and everyone was already there, she walks in. She's wearing this pink chiffon dress and her hair is up and she looks kind of different. And her date is totally gorgeous, like movie-star gorgeous. Everybody is in shock. They couldn't figure out who he was and how she got him. The guy sweeps her onto the dance floor. He holds her close and kisses her when they dance. Everybody is like, what does he see in her? They can't believe it. And as they're dancing the girl starts changing. Her skin clears up, she looks more and more beautiful and they're doing some fancy steps. Then people notice his feet. You're not gonna believe this, but it's true. . . ." Casey paused for effect.

"Suddenly they see he's not wearing shoes. They thought he was wearing black boots, but when they looked closer, they saw . . . he had *hooves*! Real hooves, and everyone starts screaming that he's the devil. He stops dancing and walks off to the bathroom or wherever and never comes back. So they all ask the girl what's going on and she can't speak. She never says another word again."

"And what about the girl? Did she stay beautiful or go back to being ugly again?" Gena asked, going along with it.

Casey shrugged. "I don't know, my aunt didn't tell me."

"Sure," Maryann said.

"Well, it's true."

"No, it *is not*!" Maryann laughed. "It's just an urban legend. They're all over the Internet."

"Oh? Steal a computer lately?" Casey asked.

Gena watched Maryann's face go pale. "Shut it, okay, Casey?"

Casey looked only halfway apologetic. "Sorry, I didn't mean . . ."

"Just forget it."

"What?" Gena asked. Something was going on between them that she didn't understand.

"Nothing," Maryann said. "Listen, I have a story, and it doesn't really matter if it's true or not because it's just scary.

"This girl goes to a graveyard on a dare. There's a big marble statue of a man sitting on a big marble chair over one of the graves, his hands resting on the chair arms like he's relaxing. The dare is for her to climb up and leave a red lipstick kiss on his big white marble lips. She has to go at night and her friends will check to see if she left the kiss the next morning.

"The next day they go over to meet her at her house but she's not home. Her mom answers the door and lets them in, and when the girl's friends realize she's missing the mom starts freaking out. The friends go down to see if she's still there. They figure she fell asleep—or she's playing a joke on them. When they walk up, they see the statue right away—it's right in the front—and sure enough, there's a big smudge of red lipstick on the guy's face. But there's also something else. The girl is there, too, sitting on his lap. Only now instead of those hands being on the chair arms, they're wrapped around their friend's body, holding her tight. She's sitting there wearing bright red lipstick, and she's stone dead."

When Maryann finished, she squinted seriously, slowly turning to look at each girl.

"Pretty good," Casey conceded. "But."

"But what? It's true, I swear," Maryann said solemnly, putting her hand on her heart. "You can still see her skeleton. Nobody was able to pry his marble hands off her!" She and Casey burst out laughing, but Gena started to feel creeped out. It should have been cozy, with the fire crackling. In fact, it *was* cozy, but she felt uneasy. The stories were completely lame, urban legends, like Maryann said. But deep down she started feeling scared. Here they were in this house in the middle of nowhere, surrounded by woods, and nobody even knew they were there. What if something happened? Cell phone, she reminded herself. Casey had a phone. They could call for help.

"How about the girl who goes for a drink of water at night and doesn't come back," Maryann was saying, still on a roll. "So her roommate goes down in the dark kitchen and feels around. She touches her friend's shoulder but the friend doesn't say anything. So she feels around and there's no head. It's just the body standing in the kitchen." Maryann gave a wicked cackle.

"Did anyone win yet?" Gena asked, sort of hoping they'd stop.

"No one wins because no one told a real story," Casey said. "But I've got one. It's real, I mean really real, not some legend, and it takes place right here at the lake."

"I don't know if we need to hear this," Maryann said, and Gena couldn't have agreed more. But Casey went on anyway.

"There's an old plantation here that's haunted. It's way over by the east side of the lake. You sometimes hear voices and moans coming from it. Maybe the water carries the sound. A couple of times a year, always around the same time, there are sounds of a big party going on there—people talking, music playing. Lots of people have heard it; everybody knows about it. My parents and their friends went out once and waited in the woods and they actually heard it too. They said it was like being in the middle of a huge celebration, only no one was there except them. Other times, you can hear crying, and people say it's the weeping of slaves who were kept in the cellar. Or you can see these dark figures moving around in what used to be the family graveyard. But if you get close they just turn into smoke.

"Once in a while, if you look up at the highest window, a round one at the top of the house, you can see a woman's face staring down. She stands there and you swear her dark eyes can see you, that she has a face full of hate and evil. People say that if you stare back at her too long, she can put a curse on you."

There was silence until Maryann said, "Awesome. You win the prize."

Gena couldn't help shivering. "How far away is this plantation?"

"Not real close, don't worry," Casey replied. "But it truly is haunted."

"What's that?" Maryann whispered suddenly, grabbing Gena's arm.

Gena jumped a mile. "What?"

Maryann made a horrified face. "That moaning sound I hear coming from the kitchen drain!"

"Shit, Maryann!" Casey cried.

"We'll all be hearing things if we keep this up."

"I really did hear something before," Gena said.

"Don't tell me, it's a voice in the toilet, right?" Casey said, making a disgusted face.

"No. I mean before, when we were out in the woods. Do you think someone could be around?"

"Somebody around outside?" Casey asked. She was tempted to mention Lane, if only to make herself feel better. Talking about the plantation had made her feel unexpectedly spooked. She really wanted to see Lane, but the idea that he might be outside right this minute was kind of scary.

"What we need to do," Maryann said, taking charge,

"is check it out. Otherwise, we'll never get any sleep. Come on."

Reluctantly, Casey and Gena followed her to the kitchen. Casey got a big flashlight out of a drawer and unlocked the door for the girls to step outside. The fire had died. The lighted windows cast weak squares on the grass. Beyond them was inky blackness. The stars were visible above, but starlight wasn't enough to penetrate the dark of the surrounding woods. Gena thought it was the darkest night she'd seen. No streetlights, no traffic, nothing to make you feel like people were around, nothing to make you feel like you weren't all alone.

As Casey shined the light from side to side, Maryann suddenly yelled, "Come out, come out, wherever you are!" Casey almost dropped the flashlight.

"Thanks! I just about peed my pants," she complained, laughing nervously.

"*Whoooo*," something called into the night.

"That owl again," Gena said when it was Maryann who jumped. "No more telling scary stories."

"Yes, Mommy," Casey replied, saving face.

They were giggling when they heard more sounds. *Swoosh, swish, crack, thump.* It wasn't funny anymore. They shrieked and ran back to the lighted doorway, crashed through it, and slammed it shut. But after a moment, they broke into laughter again.

Somehow the mood changed and they felt different toward each other, quieter, more considerate, as if they had become the friends they hadn't been before. It was like all the tension in the air had cleared the moment they were inside the warm, lighted cabin, laughing together.

They made green tea, set out mugs, found sugar and cookies, all working together, keeping their voices low. As the evening wore on, the girls settled down for the night.

Over tea, they began talking, letting down their guards. As if sharing would draw them closer and keep the fearsome things of the night out.

Maryann told them how her father had threatened her about stealing from the mall. Casey seemed to know something about the situation, but it was news to Gena. She wondered where Maryann found the nerve to walk out with three pairs of jeans but figured it probably wasn't the first time something like that had happened.

Casey started telling them about a crush she had on a guy who worked at the country club. How her parents didn't like him. Gena thought she could sense something behind Casey's words, some doubt about the guy's feelings, an uneasiness about him.

This was confession time, but what did she have to confess? Gena thought. She missed her dad sometimes, but it made her mother angry if she talked about him.

It got late, and somehow, there in the isolated cabin, late seemed much later than it did at home. Still, nobody wanted to go to sleep. On a kind of silent agreement, they went upstairs, grabbed pillows and blankets, and brought them back down to spread makeshift beds on the living room floor, in front of the fire. Nobody suggested turning off the lights.

CHAPTER 14

Moving through the dark, he felt lost. Not lost in the woods, but lost inside his head. No reasons for doing things here. Before, there was always a reason. His daddy would tell him, we're doing this for a reason. Things were clear. Now, only the dark pressing against his eyes. The angry feeling was still in him, but not as bad as before.

Things were changing. Making noise, for one thing. He was becoming different. He had never made noise before. Daddy said no noise. He wanted silent feet. Glide over the ground like a big cat, see in the dark.

Now he stumbled more than once, bumped into trees. What was happening to him? He made noise and people heard. Screechy chirping sounds like the birds he and Daddy caught. Noise would get you into trouble.

You bring it on yourself, Daddy said. *You do that, you bring it on yourself.*

Keep quiet. Say nothing. Be a monkey. See no evil, hear no evil, speak no evil. *Keep your mouth shut, you stupid oaf!* He told himself to walk very softly. To make himself invisible.

Chapter 15

Gena woke with a start, her heart racing. She sat up, ready to run, until she realized where she was. They had fallen asleep with all the lights blazing in the living room. Nobody had drawn the curtains—not that they would be much help, they were just flimsy things. From inside, the windows were mirrors, reflecting the room. But from outside, the room would be a lighted picture, framed by the night. Anybody could look in. She reached up and snapped off the nearest lamp. There were others, and the overhead kitchen light was on too. She wanted to get up to turn everything off but she was too scared to walk past the windows. They were like creepy eyes looking in at her.

This is stupid, she told herself. But she didn't move.

Had they locked the door? For that matter, how many doors were there?

She looked at Casey and Maryann sleeping and wished she could be oblivious too. She had to get up. She forced herself to stand up and quickly ran to the other lamps and clicked them off, then to the kitchen, which was brighter than anything, and flipped the switch. Darkness enveloped the rooms. Safe now.

But it was so dark without anything lit outside. The darkness was blinding. She could hardly see her way now. She stumbled, hit her toe, then stopped and held her breath, as if someone, something, was listening.

She stood there between the kitchen and living room, her eyes trying to adjust, her ears screaming with the silence. Why had the woods gone so quiet? Where were the cicadas, the frogs, the owls, all the things that should be making noise out there? She longed for the sound of a passing car.

It wasn't a car she heard. It was something else, a soft rustling sound like leaves moving. The wind, she hoped. Then a sharp snap and her heart gave a leap.

She stood motionless, afraid to make the slightest movement. She looked toward the window and realized that since the lights were off, she could see out now. She saw movement, a dark shadow moving against other shadows. Her instinct was to *disappear,* burrow into a hole, so deep that no one would know she existed at all. Instead, she was frozen, unable to move.

The shadow stopped, then moved again, coming closer to the window, as if to get a better look inside.

That was when Gena closed her eyes, afraid to see the

face that might appear through the glass, to see something looking in at her. Would it smile, growl, show its teeth? The horrific possibilities careened through her mind like a thousand screams for help.

A very long time passed—at least, that was what it felt like—and slowly she opened her eyes and dared to look. The shadow had gone.

CHAPTER 16

It was simple enough to get the number for a newspaper but not so easy to get in touch with a reporter. When the phone was picked up, Ben Jay took a deep breath. But before he could speak, a disembodied voice was asking him questions and telling him to push numbers. In desperation, he just hung on until a tired voice asked if it could help.

"I'd like to speak to Megan McCauley? She's a reporter for your paper?"

The voice told him to *hold please*. After a lot of clicks, someone barked, "Grayson, desk!"

Ben Jay repeated his request.

"We don't have any McCauley here."

"But she wrote an article—"

Grayson cut him off. "She's probably a stringer."

"A stringer?" Ben Jay was already pretty intimidated by calling a newspaper. This Grayson person wasn't helping things.

A big grunt. "Works freelance, covering stories for us in the field. What're you calling for? This personal?" Grayson sounded disapproving, like if it *was* personal there was no way he was giving out any information.

"No, no. I read one of her stories and I have some follow-up information." That sounded professional, Ben Jay hoped.

"Yeah? On what?"

"Uh . . . that story about the . . ." He found it hard to say over the phone; it sounded nutty even to him. "Mutilated animals?"

"What are you, another crackpot? Seen any aliens?"

Getting hot with impatience and annoyance, Ben Jay forgot his nervousness. He deepened his voice, trying to give it the weight of authority. "Listen, I'm calling from the Delonga sheriff's office. We've had an incident here."

"Aw jeez, I'm sorry," Grayson said, instantly friendlier. "You gotta understand we get a lot of nutcases calling in with half-assed sightings. That story of McCauley's brought them out of the woodwork. I apologize. What can I do for you, sir?"

Ben Jay stifled a laugh. "Well, you can put me in touch with this Megan McCauley."

"Sure thing. Hang on."

The phone was dropped and there was rustling of

paper. "Here she is, lives in Hot-lanta, heh, heh. Okay." He read off a phone number.

"Thanks a lot," Ben Jay said.

"So . . . you think you got a story there?"

In eagerness to discuss it, Ben Jay almost forgot his role, but he snapped back quickly. "Right now it's still under investigation. But you'll hear the news if there's anything to it."

"Delonga, huh?" the man said, as if eager to keep talking now.

"Gotta go," Ben Jay said. "Thanks again for your help."

"Anytime. Hey, I didn't get your—"

Ben Jay was already hanging up.

It was sort of late, but a reporter would always be open for information, right? Before he could lose the courage, he punched in the number he had been given.

He counted the rings, his stomach nervous. Then he heard the rollover to voice mail. He hadn't even thought out what he was going to say! He had to make his message sound right. If she'd been getting a lot of weird calls, she might not even return his.

"You've reached Megan McCauley's voice mail. She has no intention of coming to the phone right now. If you have something important to say, leave a brief message."

Nonplussed, Ben Jay tried to get his act together quickly. He gave his name and number and made his message as brief as possible. Less is more, he told himself.

"I may have something of interest regarding your story on the mutilated animals. I'm investigating a similar incident and I'd like to ask you a few questions. Please call me at your earliest convenience."

That sounded official, he hoped. He hung up. Then he waited.

CHAPTER 17

A noise. Trash woke up. For a moment, he had no idea where he was. Darkness coated his eyes like tar. His heart began racing like it wanted to get out of his chest. What?

It took a minute. Yeah, he was in the old cabin, lying on the couch. He'd been dead asleep. He told his heart to calm down. His headache was gone and he felt better, but he needed some food. He'd seen a place in the town, Linda's Diner. He'd eat something, then get the hell back home.

He got up from the couch—he was a little stiff, but nothing to worry about. He felt his way to the window, which he could see only by the difference in the degree of dark. He looked out and couldn't help feeling uneasy. It would be like stepping into a black hole out there. Then, in a momentary pulse of light from the stars, he caught a glimpse of the hood of his truck. Okay. A Plan. Get in the truck and take off. He'd be sure to keep the lake on his left or right side. That way, he wouldn't be driving around in circles. The road had to lead somewhere, take him back to that chickenshit town.

He pulled the chair away from the door and went out, feeling for his keys in his pocket. Not there. Must have left them in the truck, asshole. He opened the door and it creaked so loud it scared him. He reached over to the ignition to feel for the keys. Nothing. Must be on the floor, or maybe he dropped them on the ground. He felt for the flashlight he kept attached to the dash but the holder was empty. What was going on?

Cigarettes in his shirt pocket, his lighter. He flicked the lighter, held it up, and looked around in the weak yellow glow from the flame. Then he saw. Panic welled in his throat and the lighter fell from his hands and went out.

Glass all over the seat, the floor. The windshield was smashed. What else? He ran around to the front of the truck, using his hands to feel. One headlight gone. Gotta get out of here. He tried to open the hood but it was stuck, a dent running across, jamming it.

He pounded his fist on the wrecked truck. How could he have slept through all the noise?

For maybe a few seconds, though it felt like a long time, he ran around the truck, yelling, moaning, half crying. Then he became aware of the sounds slamming into the dark night and who knew what the hell was out there? He forced himself to shut up. Wait a minute, where was his phone? He began smacking himself all over, shirt pockets, pants pockets. Damn! Left it in the cabin. Going back inside was easier than coming out. Even though it was dark as pitch, it felt like a refuge. More feeling around on the couch, until he found the phone down between the cushions. He grabbed it, triumphant, flipped it open. His fingers were poised. Now what? Who was he going to call? It wasn't like he belonged to the fricking triple A. Call 911? He could hear them now: *What's your name? Let me see your license. Keep your hands in plain view. What's your business here?* He knew these small-town cops. Liked to hit you up for nothing. Forget it.

There was no other option. He had to walk, try to look for the lights of a house, ask for help. He shoved his phone into his pocket, went back to the open truck to retrieve his cigarettes and lighter. He thought about lighting up but changed his mind. Somehow he didn't want to be seen or heard. He crept down the road, only half guided by the darker forms of the trees and bushes on either side.

This was what it was to be blind, walking into nothing. He held his arms out, staggered a little. He could hear his feet leave the crunch of the gravel when he came out onto the lake road. Away from the truck, the cabin, he felt like sitting down in the middle of the road and crying. But he forced himself to keep walking, hands out, scared shitless, thinking any minute he would touch something and it sure as hell wouldn't be a tree.

Eventually—it must have been the reflection of the starlit sky on the lake—he could see better. He whispered, giving himself a pep talk, "Keep going keep going you gotta come to a house soon." And then he heard himself praying, of all things. He never prayed.

Then lights!

Right away he realized it was the girls: there was the red car, looking black in the dark, but he recognized it. The windows were lit up—they were awake, they'd have to help him. Shit, they knew him, right? Seen him around even if they paid him no mind. *She's a little out of your league, Macey,* he remembered someone saying.

But he was okay now, he could relax. The girls' car wasn't smashed up. Nobody had been here. Everything was fine. Walk up and knock on the door. He looked up at the window and saw her. One of them, the one with the curly hair, in a T-shirt and panties, just standing there. He could see everything she had on underneath, which was nothing. He stopped and stared, knowing she couldn't see him out there in the dark.

He was enjoying the show, until suddenly it was way weird—she was doing exactly the same thing as him, standing still and watching, looking straight out the window at him. He took a step back.

There was no way she could see him. Anyway, he wasn't doing nothing wrong. He was stranded, needing help because some shithead wrecked his truck. No sense standing there. He saw the door to the cabin, started toward it. Walked right into a wall. *Wump!* It sent him reeling. He got his bearings and looked up at something dark and bulky in front of him. A thing, a person? "Hey," he said. "I was just gonna . . ."

It was like a wall again, slamming into him, making stars in his head, lights going off at the sides of his eyes. "Hey," he said, angry now. Who was this fucker? "Whaddya think you're doing? I'm a friend here, I know these—"

There was a snuffling, a bad smell. He thought: Macey, you've run yourself right smack into a bear. He felt himself grabbed by the neck and tossed. Heard a crack of bone. Then his brain shut down.

PART TWO

Sunday

CHAPTER 18

Maryann woke up early and slipped out the kitchen door. The sun was rising and the sky was changing to soft rose and pale blue. Birds were starting to chirp. She took a deep breath of fresh air. This was wonderful, to be away, by herself, without her father breathing down her neck. She looked around at the dew-fresh grass, the sunlight glinting on the trees. The trashcan had been overturned and the grill knocked over, cold ashes spread on the ground. Raccoons, she thought, trying to scoop up the ashes with one of the dirty paper plates. Nice way to start a beautiful morning.

As she cleaned up she thought how really lonely this place was, like Casey said. But instead of seeming scary, it made her feel safe. The cabin sat in a clearing, surrounded by trees, enveloping her like a cocoon. In the back of her mind, an idea was simmering. It had begun last night when she was lying in the living room, almost asleep. Maybe she wouldn't go back. Who would miss her? Certainly not her father. There really was no reason to go back. There were a lot more reasons to stay away. All she needed was some money.

She pushed her hair out of her eyes and smiled up at the pale sun. Why couldn't every morning be peaceful like this?

Ben Jay was awakened by the phone. It was lying near him in bed, where he'd left it last night when he fell asleep waiting for Megan McCauley's call.

"Hello?"

"Is this Officer Holcomb?"

Ben Jay cleared his throat. "Yes, ma'am."

"This is Megan McCauley. You called me."

"Yes. Yes, I did."

"You awake, Officer?"

"Uh, yeah, call me Ben Jay."

"So you have information?

"Something happened here, Ms. McCauley. After I read your story, I realized that it could be connected. But I have to tell you . . . nobody here is taking it seriously. They all think it was a bear. But no way this was a bear. . . . I mean, my father . . ." It just slipped out.

And she caught it. "Ben Jay? Are you a police officer?"

The moment of truth. It was useless to keep up the pretense. "No, ma'am. My father is the sheriff. I'm sorry if I misled you but I thought—"

"That I wouldn't pay attention?" She interrupted.

"Well, yeah."

"Why don't you just tell me what happened there."

Ben Jay described it in detail as best he could, without leaving anything out. Except the key; he didn't tell her about that. She might think he was just . . . what was the term . . . grasping at straws.

There was a silence when he finished and for a moment he was scared she'd laugh.

"Ben Jay, is that cabin still the way it was, in the same condition?"

"Right now it is, but I think they're going to be cleaning it up today."

"On a Sunday? You sure?"

Ben Jay wasn't really sure. "Why?"

"I'd like to come down to take a look."

"You would do that?"

"Think you can get your father to wait?"

"If I tell him a newspaper reporter is coming, he might." But would his dad want the press in on it? He wouldn't like being made a fool of. Sometimes he got real mad when he read things in the newspaper.

"I tell you what," she was saying, "I'm going to come down to Delonga tomorrow. If you can get them to hold off cleaning until I get there, I'd appreciate it."

"I'll try. I'll tell my father."

"Good."

"Uh . . . Ms. McCauley?"

"You can call me Megan."

"Megan. If you have a minute? Could you tell me more about those things you wrote about? The fire and all, how would it be connected?"

What he had read in her article had been confusing. There had been a fire in Juniper, a small town in Tennessee, that destroyed a house on Hopecrest Street. It was after the fire that Megan had found a trail of dead animals. She had connected it to the house and the people who'd lived there.

The house had been run-down and uncared for and the fire department expected the cause to be frayed wiring, overloaded circuits—the usual hazards in an old house. A woman had been badly burned and taken to the hospital, and a man was missing. Megan had arrived when the fire was pretty much damped down, the scorched smell of it and miasma of smoke hanging over the entire street. But that was all the report had said.

"The place was full of junk from years and years," she told Ben Jay. "Piles of old newspapers and magazines, a hoard of plastic bags, phone books going back probably to when people first moved into the place. Even some old toilet seats piled up out back. It looked like they never threw anything away. People said Mr. & Mrs. Penny were like hermits, never socializing. While the firefighters were searching for Mr. Penny's body, they found a trapdoor underneath the debris on the kitchen floor. They pulled it up and climbed down and . . . well, that was when it really got interesting." Megan hesitated, as if she was considering whether to go on.

"Listen, Ben Jay, how old are you? I don't even know who I'm talking to here."

"I'm eighteen," Ben Jay lied. "I work, sort of informally, with my dad."

"Well," she said. "I guess that's old enough. It gets pretty deviant from here on, so you'll understand why I asked.

"The basement had been fixed up like a torture chamber, with iron rings fastened to the walls and chains attached to the rings. Signs of dried blood, a set of knives in a wooden rack, an axe and a saw. It had the unpleasant scent of a butcher shop. Ropes hung from the ceiling, one of them knotted like a noose. There were big foul-smelling pots, the contents boiled away, and a sticky morass on the bottom looked very suspicious. In the middle of the room was a box, looking for all the world like a coffin, with chains that could be locked around it."

Megan went on to tell him that when the search of the basement revealed no body, the firefighters were anxious to get out of there. But there was one last thing—a closet had to be checked first. The locked wooden door, charred by the blaze, had no key, but it was easy enough to break down. Inside the closet they found the missing man. He was dead, they had expected that, but fire had not caused his death. What had once been his head was a battered, pulpy mess like a smashed watermelon. They had suspected arson but that quickly turned to murder.

"When I heard this, I phoned the hospital to inquire

about the wife, who had been rescued and was in critical condition. I thought if I moved fast, I could get there before the police and ask some questions," she said.

"What'd you find out?"

"Only more questions. Mrs. Penny was under sedation, pretty groggy but obviously distressed. She kept asking me if her baby was safe. But there had been no signs of a baby in the house, no crib, no high chair, and frankly, the woman was too old to be the mother of an infant. I just figured she was delirious and maybe thinking about her child that was once a baby and now grown up. But since there were no other bodies found, I thought maybe it was this 'baby' who had bashed Mr. Penny on the head and then started the fire as a cover-up. Unfortunately, before I could find out anything more, the nurse hustled me out of there.

"I went back and talked to the neighbors. Some of them didn't know much, not having lived there long. But a few older people, residents for years, had plenty to say.

"The Pennys had had a child but he'd been sent away when he was about five or six years old, which would have been around nineteen eighty-five or -six. 'Not right,' they told me, 'something wrong in his head.' He had been sent to an institution, they weren't sure where. After he left, the incidents of missing dogs and cats ceased. Gruesome things had happened, dead dogs found with slashed and torn-up bodies, birds crushed to death. It was logical to blame the child, although he must have been very disturbed to do that kind of thing at such a young age."

"You know what that points to?" Ben Jay said, "Torturing animals is one of the three early warning signs of a serial killer. Henry Lee Lucas and Jeffrey Dahmer both did it."

"You certainly know your stuff," Megan commented.

Ben Jay was on a roll. "Another one of the behaviors is starting fires. Which Son of Sam did."

"Whoa, whoa," Megan said. "All of that might be documented, but you're forgetting one thing. There are only animals on this trail I've been following, no human victims."

"What about the father? Doesn't he qualify as a human victim?"

"That was different. To say something really bad was going on in that house is an understatement. But there's no proof the boy was part of it. He might have killed his father in self-defense, or out of fear. After that, he was back to killing animals."

"Except for the father, there were no people killed?"

"There were some disappearances in the town in the late eighties. A young woman who didn't come back from jogging, a girl who never returned from a dance. But they seemed to have nothing to do with the boy. He was only eight and he hadn't been there. But there was definitely a connection between the animals and the boy. There were animal killings before he was sent away, and again when he might have come back. One of the people I talked to said she saw Mr. Penny with a young man from time to time."

"So the son *did* return!" Ben Jay exclaimed. "That could be him out there now."

"Possibly. The thing that's a fact is that after people thought the boy was back, animals did start turning up dead. But no one actually saw him doing anything. I started thinking about the women too. There were a few more cases but in a different town. The most significant thing is that after the fire, the trail of dead animals started moving, and to tell the truth, I wasn't prepared for what I found.

"Missing dogs from trailer parks. A badly mauled horse, parts of which had been ripped out in a pattern that suggests it was eaten. And a lot of sheep. People were upset. There was talk of UFOs, goatsuckers, satanic cults, ritual death. There's a path, if anyone bothers to look, straight from Hopecrest Avenue to Georgia. And now, it seems, right to Delonga."

"Sheep . . ." Ben Jay was thinking aloud. "There was a killer called the Monster of Dusseldorf who also stabbed sheep, along with human victims."

"I have to remind you again, Ben Jay, we are talking only about animals. Dogs, cats, sheep, horses, whatever." With that, her tone became brisk and businesslike. "Now, all this has been very interesting, but we'll have to finish this conversation when I get to Delonga. Give me directions and I'll let you know when I get to town."

"What were they doing in the torture chamber?" Ben Jay couldn't help asking.

"Torturing," Megan said simply. "Definitely something sick. Look, I really have to go."

Ben Jay could sense her urgency. Though he had what seemed like a hundred questions, he put them aside and gave her directions. He promised he'd make his father delay the cleanup. When he hung up he sat and thought. Then he grabbed a pen and a yellow pad and started making notes.

There was definitely a pattern in the mutilated animals. And a connection. When the kid was sent to the loony bin, the animal massacres stopped, Ben Jay reasoned. Then he gets out, and they start again. He doesn't seem to be staying in one place too long; he doesn't want to be caught. He's following the mountains and rural areas and staying away from big towns and cities. Ben Jay pictured the woods, the lonely places around the lake, the swamps. The old cabins were a ready-made shelter for someone trying to hide.

There had to be some humans in there somewhere, he was convinced. Or else this was one very weird serial killer.

Slowly, Trash became aware of the sounds of morning. His first feeling was relief. The night and the nightmare were over. He opened his eyes to a patch of blue sky above him.

It took him a second to figure it out. He was lying on

his back, on the ground. As he shifted position, he could hear the crunch of dry leaves, smell the damp. He was lying outdoors, in the woods, on the ground, leaves covering his body like a blanket.

He tried to sit up and pain hit him like a load of bricks, across his eyes, in the back of his head, in his back. His stomach turned over and bitter fluid came up into his mouth. He had to lie down again. Think.

The nightmare. Some of it must have been real. But not all of it; couldn't be. Nothing like that could be real. He thought he was gonna die last night. And maybe somebody figured he was dead, because it sure looked like they'd tried to bury him. Get up, he told himself, get to the truck, make tracks out of here.

Then he remembered. The truck was trashed. Trash's truck trashed. He tried a laugh but it hurt too much. Why had he ever thought of following those chicks? What a fucked-up idea. Still lying on his back, he turned his head, expecting to see the cabin where he'd found the girls. Instead, there was nothing but woods, bushes; no signs of life. Except me, he thought. Left for dead, but alive anyway.

He was right back to where he started last night, only now he didn't have a truck and he'd have to walk to town. And now—there was no getting away from it—he would have to tell the cops because no way was he letting somebody get away with this. Cops could see for themselves his truck had been done. And him too; he didn't beat his own self up, did he? Anger gave him the strength to sit up. When he put his hand to the back of his head, it came away sticky with blood.

He stood up and nausea immediately hit, the world began to spin and he gagged. He leaned on a tree, waited until it passed. He was surrounded by woods. No trail, no road in sight. Which way to go? Even though he was about to puke, he felt around in his pockets for his cigarettes. Gone. His shirt was torn, his belt had been pulled out of his pants loops. Great, he would have to walk to town holding his pants up. He started forward, willing himself to take one step at a time, the pain just about killing him. His eyes felt like they were about to pop out.

He made slow progress, pushing at the undergrowth. Maybe he should think about praying again, although last night's miracle had come with a price.

God? Help me out here?

A few more steps. Stop and take a breath. Beat down the puke. Another step. There on the ground was his belt. Chewed up at one end. He picked it up anyway, pulled it through the loops and buckled it. Small thing like that made him feel better, more normal. Gritting his teeth, he stumbled on.

Lonnie Crane had come in late, then had a hard time getting to sleep. He was so worked up, he thought he'd sleep till noon. But here he was, eyes wide open before dawn. Still excited. Wondering if it had all really happened.

But his knuckles were bruised, his hand was aching,

and there was blood on his pillow. He could still taste the blood in his mouth. You couldn't deny the evidence. It had happened.

He sat back, and a slow, sly smile spread across his face.

CHAPTER 19

The flat-bottomed bateau slipped through the cola-colored water of the lake in near silence. Casey was pleased with herself for being able to rig up the electric motor and get it started. She tilted her face to the sun. "This is great, isn't it?"

They were on their way to the cabin where Lane would be with his friends. Of course, Gena and Maryann didn't know about their destination. She'd just talked them into taking a boat ride across the lake.

"I could live like this all the time," Maryann said, trailing her hand in the water.

"It's so peaceful," Gena agreed dreamily. After her momentary panic last night, she'd fallen into a deep sleep. This morning, with the sun streaming in, the whole idea of being so scared seemed stupid.

"You know what I said last night, about my father

and all?" Maryann asked. "I'm thinking that maybe I won't go back home."

"What do you mean?" Gena was confused. "What would you do?"

It got Casey's attention too. "And where would you go?"

Maryann shrugged. "Ever since my mama died, I've been taking care of myself, and him. I do all the shopping and cooking and cleaning. Even have to wash his dirty socks. I know how to take care of myself."

"But you can't just disappear. He'd find you," Gena said.

"You really think he cares?"

"Well . . . he might *have* to care, like if the school started wondering where you were and social services got involved. They'd *make* you come back."

"They couldn't," Maryann said. She knew her father would want her back, no doubt about it. He'd miss her, all right—anyone would miss having a maid 24/7.

"He's your father," Casey insisted. "He can make you do whatever he wants."

Gena thought of her own father, what her Mom had said about alcohol, how it was considered abuse. Lots of words had been flying around back then. You didn't have to live with someone who abused you. "Maybe they'd find you another place to live," she said to Maryann.

"What? Like a foster home? Forget that."

Maryann could be so tough, but how could she live

by herself? The idea intrigued Gena. What would it be like not to have to be nagged so much about everything?

"So where would you go?" Casey asked. "Like hypothetically."

"Like hypothetically, I'd go to a big city. Only that's probably a bad idea because all runaways think they can make it in a city and all that happens is they turn into druggies or prostitutes."

"Sounds like you already know a lot about it," Casey said snidely.

"Read a book or watch the news, Casey," Maryann snapped back.

"So where *would* you go?" Gena asked, wanting to smooth things over.

"Some town far away, not too big or too small, a place where I could get a job and just blend in. Be a waitress, find a room, live normal."

Gena pictured Maryann arriving in a small town, getting off the bus. In a movie, there would be soothing music to let you know it was going to be okay. Maryann would walk down a tree-lined main street and find a Victorian-looking rooming house. The grandmotherly woman who ran it would say she could stay without paying rent until she got a job. In the next scene, Maryann would be wearing a pink uniform, taking orders on a pad, smiling at the customers in a diner. Before the movie ended, she would meet a handsome and rich man who would ask her to marry him. As if things like that could happen in real life. Gena was too practical. She couldn't see how it would be easy to run away and live a normal life.

"You'll see," Maryann said, as if reading her mind.

I've already run away, Gena thought. And this is nothing compared to what it would be like if I really took off on my own. She could imagine having panic attacks and feeling alone and guilty. She wasn't cut out for it, that was all. She'd just plod along until whatever happened, happened in her life. One thing she knew, she wasn't getting married anytime soon. If somebody asked her what her secret dream was, if she could have any wish she wanted, she'd say she wanted to go live in Paris. She saw herself sitting in a sidewalk café, drinking a café au lait and reading a book.

Casey's mind was elsewhere, though not far from Gena's. She was thinking about living with Lane. He'd work at the country club, and she'd have dinner ready when he came home. Then they'd go into the bedroom. Or maybe before dinner. She couldn't get the vision going, though. There was something missing in it, but she wasn't quite sure what.

"Look," Maryann said suddenly, interrupting the quiet mood that had decended, "there's a perfect spot for a picnic." She pointed to the shore to their right, a smooth bank of green grass scattered with tiny flowers, overhung with willows.

"It looks like a fairy tale," Gena said, in the mood for fantasy. "Let's head over there."

"We can't," Casey said. They looked at her.

She gave a small nervous giggle. "There's no place to get out of the boat. We'd get soaked."

"Is there a problem?" Maryann asked, waggling her Nikes at Casey. All of them were wearing jeans and running shoes. Nothing to worry about if they got wet.

"You don't know anything about boats," Casey said, her eyes fixed on the far shore.

"Well excuse me, captain." Maryann looked at Gena. "What do you think? Should we have a mutiny? Or is it mutinize?"

"I'm serious," Casey said, her face set. Nobody was going to interfere with her plan to see Lane.

"Somebody's got a wild hair up her whatsit," Maryann said.

Casey ignored her. "That's where we're headed," she said, pointing toward the farther shore, where Lane's cabin would be. "See? There's a dock."

"See? There's a dock, Gena," Maryann mimicked. "Can't get off the boat without a dock."

Casey just kept aiming for it.

"Hey. What's up?" Maryann suddenly tuned in. She looked more closely at Casey, who was intently navigating the boat to shore. "Is this what I think it is?"

"What?" Gena asked, confused.

"Suddenly I have a strong feeling that Casey's made some plans she didn't tell us about."

"Plans?"

"Yeah, Casey, what's the plan? Wait, Wait! Don't tell me. Could there be a person on that distant shore by the name of Lane?"

"We're just going to say hello, that's all. Lane just happened to be staying here this weekend."

"And you just *happened* to know?" Maryann said.

"He's here with two friends. . . ."

"Oh great. You fixed us up? We're gonna spend the week with blind dates? What the hell? Casey?" Maryann looked thoroughly annoyed.

"No, you're not spending the week with them. Look, I thought if I told you ahead of time you might not want to come up here."

"*That's* why you asked me?" Gena said, incredulous. So much for anything like friendship. "You're just using me to see *him*?"

"Of course I'm not. I thought we could all have some fun."

"So who are these dudes?" Maryann asked, the curiosity in her voice suggesting a change of tune. She was now gazing almost eagerly toward shore.

"Lane's friends, I met one of them, Jeff. I don't know the other one."

"Not Jeff with the ponytail!" Maryann screeched. She and Casey laughed together.

Maryann doesn't mind at all, Gena thought. But what about me? I've never even met this Lane person Casey's always talking about. Gena had the impression he was sort of rough. Older.

"Why didn't they call or come around last night?" Maryann was asking.

"We're a surprise," Casey admitted, looking at the shore a little nervously now. Maryann picked up on it.

"Oh. But they *are* here on their own, right? I mean, there's no chance they brought their own dates with them?"

A flicker of doubt crossed Casey's face. "Of course not. They came up here to go fishing."

"And we all know that fishing is a man thing," Maryann pressed harder.

"Lane didn't say anything about dates," Casey said doggedly.

Maryann winked at Gena. "Well, let's hope the big surprise isn't on us!"

"Oh, shut up," Casey snapped. She headed for the dock, pulling the boat in neatly. The cabin was perched at the top of the short rise. It looked quiet and deserted. She prayed that the boys were really there. Then the door cracked open. Lane put his head out, saw them, and came running down the hill. Gena heard Casey's big sigh of relief as she waved to him. "Hey, Lane!"

But Lane didn't wave back and he wasn't smiling. He looked worried. "Casey? Is that you?"

To Gena's ears, it sounded like he was disappointed.

It took the wind out of Casey. "Yeah. It's me."

Gena was embarrased for Casey. She was embarrassed for herself. Casey had been stupid not to let them know they were coming. She should have called to be sure it was all right. They probably *did* have their own dates, or else it was some big stag thing and they didn't want female company.

When Lane reached the dock, the four stood for a moment in awkward silence. Then Maryann had to ask, "What's wrong?"

"Forget it," Casey whispered to her, "let's just push off again."

Lane shook himself, as if getting his bearings. "Sorry, we thought . . . we thought you were Jeff. We've been waiting for him." He paused, looking around distract-edly. "You better come on up."

"I don't think so," Casey said coldly.

"No, really, come on."

Casey was trying to make up her mind. Gena thought the good idea would be to just leave, save what was left of their dignity. But Maryann was giving Casey a gentle shove forward.

"We're sorta worried," Lane was saying. "Jeff took a walk and he hasn't come back."

Casey looked at Gena and Maryann as if to say *so what's the big deal?* "Well, it's still early. He probably got lost. It's easy to get mixed up and go around in circles out there."

Lane looked directly at her. "No, you don't understand. He went for a walk *last night*. He's been gone since then."

They took this in, not knowing what to say until Lane broke the silence. "Come on, Bailey's making coffee."

They followed him up the hill. In the cabin, a tall,

handsome, brown-haired boy was pouring hot water into mugs. "Hey, ladies," he said. "Would you like coffee or tea? I'm making some chai."

After a good ten minutes of small talk, they stood around holding their mugs, stirring and blowing on the drinks to cool them off, not quite knowing what to do next. Casey walked around the room, looking as if she expected hidden dates to pop out.

"You sure he didn't come back? Like when you were all asleep?" Maryann asked.

Lane gave an emphatic yes, but Bailey shook his head. "Well it's in the realm of possibility. We can't be absolutely sure, since we were sleeping. But that would mean he went back out again this morning."

Maryann was walking around the room. "So I guess he didn't leave a note?"

Gena wondered why they were all standing there drinking coffee and tea. "Shouldn't you be out looking for him?" That came out wrong. Maybe she should have said *we*. It looked like they were now involved, whether they wanted to be or not.

"We did look," Lane said. "But"—he gestured with his arms—"these woods are so big, we didn't really know where to start."

Casey seemed annoyed. She took a cigarette out of a pack on the kitchen banquette and lit it. "He'll come back," she said, flopping the lighter onto a table. "And if y'all go out and he comes back, then he'll start worrying about *you*."

"We think he had an accident," Lane said. "He could be stranded out there. Listen, Casey, you know these woods, right? You told me you've been coming up here since you were born. You could help, show us where to search."

Casey just stood there. Gena thought this would be a great opportunity for Casey to shine for Lane—now was her chance to impress him. But she just kept smoking and looked downright sulky.

Maryann walked over and stood in front of her, staring her down. "Come on, Case, don't be a bitch."

"Okay, okay." She stubbed out the cigarette. "There's a road that goes up to the old cabins. It's pretty overgrown. If Jeff went up there, he'd get lost for sure. And nobody stays up there anymore, so no one would be around to help."

"Good. Then that's where we'll go," Lane said, looking relieved and grateful to have something constructive to do.

Bailey grabbed a backpack and some bottles of water. As they started out, Gena felt the mood change. It was becoming almost festive—almost like they were going on an adventure. Lane had his arm around Casey now. They all felt it: they would find Jeff, no sweat.

CHAPTER 20

Ben Jay heard water running in the bathroom, then caught the scent of his father's aftershave. He was up pretty early for a Sunday morning. If he was planning to clean the cabin today, Ben Jay would have to stop him. But when he went out to the kitchen, his father's face was grim. He was sipping a cup of black instant coffee, his phone at his ear.

"What's up, Dad?" Ben Jay asked as soon as the sheriff was done talking.

"Last night it was that poodle. This morning it's more serious. Boy gone missing now."

"Who?"

"Billy Pope. You probably know him from school."

"Yeah. I do. What happened?"

"Don't know what happened. Mother looked in his

room, the bed's not been slept in. The front door was still on the latch, waiting for him to come in last night. His car's gone. Never showed up."

Pope, that badass. Probably got drunk. Ben Jay took a half gallon of milk out of the fridge and sat down across from his father. "Where'd he go last night?"

"On a date. That Norleen number. You know her?" The sheriff shook his head "Ben Jay, how many times I told you to drink out of a glass?"

"Fine." Ben Jay went to get a glass, poured in the milk. He wondered if his father would remember seeing Lonnie heading onto Lake Road last night. He decided not to say anything.

"What about Norleen? Did she come home?" He had a thought. "Maybe they ran off, eloped."

The sheriff frowned in disapproval. "Let's be serious here. Billy's mother called over to Norleen's early this morning, worried there'd been an accident. Norleen was in bed, sleeping like a baby."

That meant Lonnie hadn't trailed them to make a fuss or get in a fight. Pope was probably parked somewhere, sleeping it off. It was well known that Pope liked a cold beer or two or four. He'd been up for a DUI last month but conveniently got off, his granddaddy being the judge.

"Well, I'm outta here," the sheriff said, putting his mug into the sink. "See you when I see you."

"Bye, Dad."

As soon as his father was gone, Ben Jay hit speed dial

for Lonnie, who answered immediately, sounding like he was expecting the call.

"You hear about Pope?"

"Pope? What about him?"

"Didn't get home last night."

There was a silence. "Well, he . . . you know, he . . ."

"What?"

"I don't know! Why're you asking me?"

"I'm not *asking* you, I just thought you'd be interested, that's all. I mean, you *were* following him all day yesterday. You see anything happen to him?"

"No! Why would I?"

"You go back to the lake looking for him after you dropped me off?"

"Course not, I went home like I said I was."

"My dad thought he saw you turning in to the lake."

"Must have been mistaken. Wasn't me. I got home, had supper, took a shower, watched some TV, then went to bed."

It was a lie. Lonnie was giving too much information. His dad always said that the liars, the guys with the phony stories of where they were and what they did, they gave you way too many details. If you had a real alibi, you didn't need to embellish. And if Lonnie supposedly turned around and went home, why'd he sound so uptight about it?

"His mother reported him a missing person. I'm hoping he stays that way," Ben Jay said, trying to cheer Lonnie up.

"I don't know where he's at," Lonnie said, his voice strained. "Listen, I gotta go."

"Lonnie, I—" Ben Jay started, but Lonnie had already disconnected.

Strange.

CHAPTER 21

They had been trudging through the woods for at least half an hour, shouting variations of "Jeff!" "Hey, buddy," and "Can you hear us?"

So far, nothing.

"You really think he would go all this way in the dark?" Maryann asked skeptically as the group followed Casey up the old dirt track.

"He had a flashlight," Bailey said.

"I don't think he could see enough with a flashlight," Lane cut in. "He could be far away from where he started."

A fish crow cawed high in the trees, making the woods seem lonelier. Gena began to doubt they could find anything at all in this dense forest. Casey looked stone bored. She had probably imagined that they'd walk a short ways and find Jeff with a broken ankle, and then she could be a hero and Lane would be impressed.

To be honest, that was what Gena had imagined herself. But now, she felt the same as Maryann. She didn't think Jeff could have walked this far or gotten this lost. It was beginning to feel creepy to her. How could he just disappear?

Casey lit yet another cigarette. She was scattering butts behind them like Hansel and Gretel with their bread crumbs. "You know, he shouldn't have gone out alone in the dark in the first place," she said. "What did he think he was doing?"

"Actually, he was saving a dog," Bailey said. "I know it sounds crazy, but Jeff heard this dog yipping and he got worried it was hurt. We told him it was probably nothing, but he wouldn't listen, he wanted to see for himself."

"And you weren't worried when he didn't come back?" Maryann asked. "What's with you guys?"

They didn't answer, just looked at each other. Finally, Lane said, "We were . . . a little out of it."

Maryann gave them an *I knew it* look.

"We only had a couple of brewskis each," Lane began.

"How time flies when you're having fun," Maryann said sarcastically.

"How could you get that drunk from two beers?" Gena asked, and Maryann gave a snort.

"Two beers and a couple of joints," she said.

"They were on vacation, okay, *Mom*?" Casey cut in, defending Lane.

Maryann was fed up. She could've forgiven Casey for

pulling one of her tricks if they had met up with the guys, hung out, and had some fun. But she really wasn't in the mood for being on a rescue team and going on a ten-mile hike. It was too bad that Jeff was lost, but it wasn't her fault. She was relieved when she spied one of the old cabins Casey had been babbling about.

She pointed through the trees. "Look! Maybe he's in there."

She hoped he was—alive or dead, who cared, so long as they found him. She went on ahead, making her way through the weeds, thinking about ticks and spiders. She stopped at a broken window and peered in. Grunge. Old furniture, cobwebs, spiders for sure. Let them look in there, she thought, walking around to the back of the cabin. There was a low humming, buzzing sound. And she almost stepped into a reddish brown puddle covered with what looked like a million flies. Underneath the undulating, buzzing mass, there was something that might have been an animal. She made out patches of pink fur that must have once been white, a long thin bone.

"Omigod," she said, thinking she was yelling but it came out as a whisper. "Hey!" she said, louder this time. "Hey! Guys!"

They came running, expecting to see Jeff.

"It's only a dog," Lane said.

The poor thing, Gena thought. She reached down to pick up a red collar studded with rhinestones. "This must be the dog Jeff heard last night."

Casey was holding her nose. "What happened to it?"

"Something got it," Lane said.

"Gator?" Bailey asked.

"Too far from the lake," Casey said.

"But what else would do something like this?" Maryann asked.

"A wild boar?" Bailey suggested.

Gena was shaking her head. She had seen something that gave her chills. A crude attempt had been made to bury the dog's body. It was lying in a shallow trough covered with leaves. Animals didn't dig graves. "A boar didn't do this. It was human."

"Oh, come on—" Casey started, but Gena broke in.

"Just look, Casey."

"No thanks, one look was enough."

"Does it matter?" Maryann asked. "Instead of arguing, we should get out of here. Haven't you ever seen a movie? Whatever killed the dog might still be around." She turned to Lane and Bailey. "Y'all are gonna have to do what you should have done before, call the police. Why didn't you do it last night?" She made an exaggerated pause. "Oh, that's right. You didn't want to get busted."

"Now *you're* the one being bitchy," Casey said to her as they turned around to start back.

"Well, it doesn't look like anybody's in the mood to party, does it?" Maryann was determined to get the last word in.

"Can you two just cut it out!" Gena cried. Were they

going to bicker the whole week? She rubbed her arms at the sudden chill in the air and noticed that the sky had darkened. That was all they needed—a storm. She stomped off ahead of them, thoroughly fed up.

Bailey quickly caught up with her. "Bad vibes back there, huh?"

But Gena didn't answer—she was hearing something else. A slow dragging sound from the woods, the sharp snap of a twig. She stopped, put her hand up to alert Bailey. They stood and listened to the sound of snuffling and snorting. Maryann had been right; the animal *was* still hanging around. Bailey turned and held up his hand to warn the others. Casey made a face, asked, "Now what is it?" but Lane shushed her. Suddenly everyone could hear it, something large and violent.

"What *is* that?" Gena whispered to Bailey.

He gave her a look. "You're asking *me?* Nobody liked any of my suggestions. I'm still thinking that wild boar. And you don't want to mess with one of those."

They didn't move. It was as if all of them were trying to will the animal to go away. When the scream came, it was like they'd been hit with it—it pushed them backward, a blow that crashed into the solar plexus, took their breath, left them empty of everything but terror. Someone crying out pitifully, in pain. A human sound. They all had the same thought: Jeff. He was seriously hurt. But nobody wanted to be the first to step off the path and enter the woods.

Lane finally found his voice. "Okay, buddy," he called

out. His voice was strangled. "Hang on," he called louder. "We're on our way!" He and Bailey pushed through the underbrush, branches smacking them in the face.

"You going too?" Maryann asked Casey. Casey looked undecided.

"Come on, we have to," Gena said, and plunged into the bushes after the boys. Maryann and Casey followed her, pushing branches and stumbling over roots. Gena saw that there were faint signs of a trail. Someone had been there before them.

Then, abruptly, they all came out into a small area where the brush had been trampled down. There was torn foliage everywhere, signs of a frenzied struggle. The surrounding trees were splashed with dark spots and stains. There were dark patches on the ground. And something lying there. A body. This time human.

Like the dog, the body had been torn apart. The chest looked like it had exploded; the skin was peeled back and the ribs exposed. Gena thought it looked prehistoric, like a dinosaur skeleton in a museum. But there was no blood, just what looked like a coating of rust on the wounds. The face was battered, the mouth hanging open like it had been caught in a scream.

"He's . . . dead?" Casey asked, an unnecessary question.

The body looked *very* dead. It had been dead for a while. There was no way it could have cried out just a few seconds before. But if not, who *had* screamed?

Lane had fallen to his knees, groaning.

"What do we tell his parents?" Bailey asked in a strangled voice.

"Omigod, what are we supposed to do now?" Casey said, shaking, unable to tear her eyes away from the horrible sight, revolted yet fascinated by it.

"Call the police like you said we should have done," Lane replied.

"I never said that," she fired back. The last thing she, Maryann and Gena needed was to talk to the police.

They stood there looking at the body, and it got easier as the minutes crept by. They were drawn to it and repulsed at the same time. They hardly noticed how the wind whipped around them, sending the trees into a frenzy, then just as suddenly settled down again.

Lane made a strange sound and jumped to his feet. "Guys. This isn't Jeff."

They all stepped closer. It didn't even look human to Gena anymore. It was amazing what you could get used to.

"How can you even tell?" she asked. The face was unrecognizable. They had been looking for Jeff, and they had found a body. It was a logical to think it was Jeff. How many bodies *were* there lying around in these woods? She felt a laugh coming up into her throat like a burp and she swallowed quickly. If she laughed, she'd sound hysterical.

Lane was pointing at the body. "Belt buckle," he said. "Jeff wasn't wearing that thing." The buckle glistened with something Gena didn't want to think about, certainly not polish. It was a big brass skull with slanted, evil-looking eyes, wearing a crown.

Relief made them all want to laugh, but the sounds came out sounding garbled—almost demented—and they all shut up again. Still, they had a reason to be happy, didn't they? It wasn't Jeff, which meant Jeff wasn't dead. Which meant he was alive. Maybe at this very moment he was back at the cabin, worrying about them.

It was nice that it wasn't Jeff, but it was *someone*, Gena thought. And whoever killed him couldn't be far away. Where was that person now? They had heard the screaming and crying just moments before. She looked around and could see that it was a thought in all of their minds.

"Let's get out of here," she said urgently.

Her fear infected the others and they all began to run.

CHAPTER 22

Lane had his cell out as they were making their way back. "What do I do? Call 911?"

Casey snatched the phone away from him so fast, he was left with his hand out, empty, and a stunned look on his face.

"You're not calling anybody until we're out of here."

Lane grabbed his phone back. "Have you gone nuts?"

"You can't," she said, calming down. "We're not supposed to be here. Wait until we leave and then call. Or drive into town and talk to them in person. Just don't mention anything about us."

"But you were with us when we found the body, they'll ask—"

"It doesn't matter if we were there or not," Maryann broke in. "The cops don't have to know. We had nothing to do with him. You don't even know him! We're not connected, so forget we were here."

She heard Casey make a small sound at that. Casey wouldn't like Lane to forget she was there, but tough shit, they were *not* getting involved.

"It doesn't seem right, you taking off like this," Bailey said. "We could use the moral support, at least."

Then Casey did something with her eyes that Maryann could not believe. She turned directly to Lane and said in a syrupy voice, "Y'all could come over to our cabin tonight for some moral support."

"You want to entertain *now*, Casey? That's just gonna call attention to us," Maryann couldn't believe Casey's thought process, but stopped herself and changed directions. "Listen, you want to blow it, go ahead." She was at least glad to see that the boys didn't seem enthused by the invitation. All she was interested in was extricating herself from any involvement with the cops.

When they finally came into view of the lake and the boys' cabin again, Lane and Bailey ran ahead, calling for Jeff. There was still the possibility that he *had* gone on an early-morning walk and had made his way home.

And as soon as the boys ran off Casey was back at it. "See? We can still have a good time. After they go to town, they can come back and we'll—" But she stopped at the sight of Lane and Bailey returning. Both looked more worried, if that was possible.

"Still no sign of him," Lane said.

Casey opened her mouth as if to start making plans

in spite of it, but Maryann said quickly, "Let's stop talking and get going."

The sky had grown darker. A zigzag of lightning suddenly sizzled across the water.

"You better let us drive you back," Bailey said.

"No, no, you need to start to town before it rains and the roads turn to mush," Casey said, to Maryann's relief. "We need to get the boat away from here. If the police come, they'll ask questions and find out it's my family's boat and wonder what it's doing over on this side of the lake." The big surprise had been a flop. Nothing had turned out the way Casey planned.

They hurried to the bateau as thunder cracked. As they moved off from the dock, the surface of the lake was pockmarked with raindrops.

"Isn't it supposed to be dangerous out in a boat in an electrical storm?" Maryann asked, looking back to where the boys were still standing on the dock. "Maybe we should let them drive us."

"Shit, Maryann!" Casey snarled. "It was you who said it wasn't a good idea to go with them."

"I wasn't talking about a ride. I meant that having them come over tonight for a party was a bad idea. A person is missing and a person is dead. The cops are going to ask them a lot of questions and maybe keep an eye on them for a while. Which means we should stay clear of them. But if it means getting electrocuted, I could handle a ride."

"Shut up! Shut up!" Gena yelled. "I can't stand listening

to you two anymore. Just try to get us back to the cabin before we all drown, okay?"

Maryann gave an exaggerated sigh. Casey just sat at the front of the boat and pouted. Gena was exhausted. They were driving her insane. Casey especially—served her right for chasing after Lane. If they hadn't gone over this morning, they wouldn't know anything about dead dogs and dead bodies.

Another flash of lightning, more thunder. Gena jumped.

"Don't freak," Casey said. "It's only rain."

As if to mock her words, the wind came up and roiled the lake, churning the water into what looked like potato soup. The bateau rocked like a paper sailboat on the rippling waves. Gena clutched at its sides. She felt even more afraid when she saw Maryann and Casey doing the same thing.

"Are we there yet?" she tried to joke.

Casey's reply was whipped away in the wind.

"What?" she yelled.

"We should be. . . ."

"We should be?" Maryann cried. "You know the way back, don't you?"

It was taking too long, Gena thought. It had been faster this morning. But then, this morning it wasn't raining, she told herself. Keep calm. Take your mind off it. Think about the dreaded meat loaf Mom makes on Friday nights, with the boiled egg in the center. Who ever invented that recipe? Think about fun stuff, like Matt asking you to pull his finger and then farting.

Someone was screaming.

Casey. The rain was a thick undulating curtain now, cutting off all sight of the shore.

"Somebody bail!"

"I'd like to bail, all right," Maryann yelled back.

Water pooled in the bottom of the boat. Bail with what? Gena could hardly see Casey now. Maryann was a vague shape with wet hair plastered down, her head looking like a skull.

The boat rocked. The motor sputtered. Then it died.

Casey's voice: "Shit!"

Maryann was half standing. "Where's the dock? Look for the dock!"

They could hardly see an inch in front of them—how were they supposed to see the dock? Gena squinted through the rain, which felt like nails being driven into her skin. The lightning looked like knives stabbing toward them. We're gonna die, be electrocuted! They always blew the whistle to get out of the pool when there was lightning!

Gena heard thumping and Casey was pushing something at her. "Here, we gotta row."

Maryann stood up and swung an oar around.

Gena felt a blow on her shoulder. Not really hard, but it made her want to cry. Like being hit was the last straw. "Watch it," she started to say, and then she was somewhere else. In the water, gulping. What happened? She couldn't get her mind to figure out what to do. Her body took over, her feet kicking, her arms moving, remembering to swim.

But the water felt thick and heavy, like moving through molasses. Her clothes pulled her down; her sneakers felt like ten-ton weights. She didn't seem to be moving anywhere. Every few seconds, the water surged into her face and she had to spit, and blink it out of her eyes.

She made an effort to stay afloat, to kick her legs even though she didn't know if she was going anywhere. Finally, vague shadows on the horizon changed into the identifiable shapes of trees. At last her feet touched bottom.

"Thank god, thank god." She said it like a mantra, dragging herself through water up to her hips, her knees, her ankles. She staggered onto the coarse sandy soil and fell.

For what seemed like minutes, she had no other thoughts than to be thankful for her life. Then she remembered Casey and Maryann. But what could she do? She lay there, the rain still coming down, still striking her like arrows. A shiver began deep inside; a tremor ran through her limbs, turning her skin to gooseflesh. She tried to stand but made it only to her knees.

"Help." A pitiful voice, no one would hear it. She felt like lying down, going to sleep.

She might have even been dozing when she heard

someone coming toward her. A flood of relief made her instantly feel warmer. They'd made it to shore—Casey and Maryann were coming to get her.

A shape loomed in the mist, bulky, hunched, too tall and wide to be one of them. Coming at her like a dark menace, blocking out her warm relief, replacing it with cold terror.

"Who?" was all she managed to whisper before everything turned wrong, upside down. Blood rushed to her head, stopped up her ears. Her head fell into space. Dizzy, bouncing, she felt herself moving. She was being carried away from the shore, into the woods.

"Wait . . . ," she tried to protest. The woods closed around her. Shimmering ebony beads danced in front of her eyes. Then she was gone.

CHAPTER 23

He moved through the woods, careful not to let the body bump into tree trunks or get caught in sticky brambles like the other one. He wouldn't hurt this one. It would be his treasure to care for and keep.

Every once in a while, the body made a sound and he had to stop. "Ssssh," he said, but it twisted and pulled, cried and said the same thing over and over: "Please-pleaseplease."

"Shut the hell up," he said, but not angrily. Noise was not on the agenda, as his father always used to say.

To stop noise, his father would hit them on the head. But that resulted in a mess, blood, sometimes not waking up for a long time. He wouldn't do that. There had to be other methods.

But the body kept repeating "pleasepleaseplease" and it got on his nerves. He had to stop it. "Noise is not on the agenda," he said in a stern voice. Then he hit it. There was a whimper, and quiet.

The rain had stopped and the trees dripped. There were no footsteps, no one was coming.

He had learned to walk softly, to breathe low, to make no sound at all. Like the Injuns, his father said, teaching him all the tricks. But sometimes, without realizing, he started making a *humhum* noise in his throat. It used to keep him company on long dark nights. He got whipped if he made it when they were on the hunt. *Humhum* was not on the agenda.

Well, no more of that. Didn't have to worry anymore. Nothing left of that but a gooey mashed-up banana.

He knew by himself that quiet was the way to survive; he didn't need teaching.

He stopped to rest. The body was quiet. The trees dripped. He was safe.

Then he moved on, careful not to let the body bump into trees. He carried it carefully to the secret place he had found. A lucky break.

When he got there, he waited to be sure no one was watching. Nobody would be out in the rain anyway, people hated rain. He was proud of finding this hiding place. It was ideal. That was a word his father liked. At home, the room they had made in the basement was ideal too. An ideal place, where you could do anything you wanted and no one would know.

He took the body down the ladder carefully. Put it in the corner, its head leaning against the wall. It was sleeping, safe and sound. But soon it would wake up and ask questions. Want food and water. It could be a problem. This one would want proper food like cereal, Big Macs, Kentucky Fried Chicken, cans of soup, pizza. But as he had learned, a problem could be solved. Think about it and the solution would come. Never give up, never say die. All he had to do was figure it out.

He sat awhile, clicking the flashlight he had found on and off, watching the body. And just like he'd thought it would, a solution came into his head.

If you wanted people food, you went to where the people were. Simple as that, easy as pie. He got up again, made sure everything was shipshape, then climbed back out of the hiding place and went to where he knew he would find the right food. He had seen it, he had smelled it, he had tasted it. The proper food. Nothing too good for my baby.

CHAPTER 24

Ben Jay was watching TV when his cell rang.

"I have some bad news," his father said. "Some kids come in here this morning and told me there's a body up in the woods near the old cabins. And I start thinking if it could be Billy Pope. You wouldn't know anything about his way of dressing? What he might wear on his belt?"

Pope dead? Some kind of accident? What was his father talking about, how Pope dressed? "What do you mean?"

"Like a belt buckle, something distinctive?"

"Oh. Yeah, that skull."

"Could you describe it?"

"Well, Dad, I don't spend that much time checking out Pope's pants, but it's some kind of scary-looking skull wearing a crown."

"That's it, then."

"You mean it's Pope?"

"Can't be one hundred percent sure until we get an identification. I'll have to ask Mrs. Pope to come down. That won't be a pleasant thing. But these boys described a buckle like that."

"What boys?"

"Couple of boys staying at the lake for some fishing this weekend. Found the body. Doesn't look good."

There was something in his father's voice. "How not good?" Ben Jay asked.

"Torn up some. Nasty."

"Torn up how? You thinking it's your ol' bear again?"

"Naw, we picked ourselves up a suspect already. Handed hisself to us on a platter, walked right up to the deputy's car. Looked like he'd been in a bad fight, covered with blood. Gave us a song and dance about losing his truck, getting attacked."

"Who was it?"

"Not from around here and not too cooperative. We're holding him on suspicion."

"You going to get Pope's body?"

"Ambulance is coming, but they won't be able to get to the spot. We'll have to go up and bring it out to the road."

"I'll come," Ben Jay said.

"Maybe you shouldn't. . . ."

"I'm coming." With this new development, it was

unlikely they would be worrying about the cabin. He could show it to Megan McCauley in its original condition. But now he was anxious to get up to the lake. This might be something else for Megan. He wondered who the suspect was. And he wondered about Lonnie.

Trash was left sitting in a cell in his underwear until some deputy named Dexter brought him an old army fatigue jacket to put on. First thing they had done was take his clothes away for evidence. Gave him back his shoes, no socks or laces, and a paper cup of coffee. The deputy told him his rights, reading them off a three-by-five card—but wasn't he supposed to get a phone call? Get a lawyer or something? The whole situation didn't seem right.

They asked a lot of questions, but he wasn't going to say nothing about spying on those girls. That was sure to sound a lot worse than it was. Followed them all the way to Delonga? That sounded suspicious even to Trash. What had he been thinking about? It was all the blonde's fault, leading him all the way to bumfuck.

"What're you accusing me of?" he'd asked.

The big ol' dumb sheriff tried to be cagey. Asked about a body in the woods. Trash had to laugh. If there had been a body in the woods, it had been his own, left for dead. He tried to explain how he'd been knocked out, didn't know what happened until this morning when he woke up and started walking to town. Woke up in a grave, for god's sake! He could see they didn't believe him about the grave. Wanted to know was he six feet under and what was the name on the tombstone.

Told them about his truck. They said they'd look for it. Didn't sound enthusiastic. He explained how he parked near a cabin, got out for a piss, took a walk. He didn't like to say he'd been inside the cabin to sleep. They'd get him for breaking and entering or some such. He hoped they wouldn't notice the lock was broke.

"Took a walk, huh?" they started in. "Where to? What for?"

He clammed up. Wasn't saying no more.

"Hey! What about a lawyer here?" he called out every few minutes. Nobody answered.

CHAPTER 25

"If she didn't drown, then where is she?" Casey asked again, standing at the window, staring out at the rain.

"I told you, she got to shore. I saw her, okay? She's probably just waiting for the rain to stop."

"She might need help." Casey was whining again.

Maryann threw down the magazine she had been pretending to read. She was cold and tired and miserable and Casey was the last person she'd have expected to overreact like this. When they had finally gotten back to the cabin, the power was out. They made a fire, but all it did was smoke and smell of tar and make the room even colder. "Just give it a little longer," she repeated for what seemed like the twentieth time.

Maryann was sure she had seen Gena up on the shore before the bateau changed direction and the fog closed in. But now she was afraid that maybe Gena had met up with the police. Once Lane and Bailey reported the body, the police would be out there. If Gena had gone off in the wrong direction, they could have picked her up. She'd be a mess; she'd have to tell them what had happened to her. Would the cops connect them with Lane and the body? At the very least, they'd call Gena's mother, and then everything would come out. It might come out anyway unless Lane and Bailey could keep their mouths shut.

"I think we need to go into town," Casey said. "If we don't, it will look worse."

"Worse than what? Our boat sank, we almost drowned, why should we be worrying about the body of someone we don't even know? You scared they'll think we murdered him?"

"Well, what do you think we should do?"

"I'm thinking I'll just get lost myself."

"Oh, Maryann, stop sounding stupid."

"I'll tell you what's stupid," Maryann retorted. "Your idea to come up here in the first place."

"It was *our* idea."

"You thought of it. You arranged it. You wanted to come because of Lane. Gena and I were props so you wouldn't have to be here alone. And look where it got you. Lane wasn't exactly thrilled to see you. It looks like the big romance was all in your mind."

Casey was shocked into silence and just stared at Maryann. Finally, she asked in a small voice, "Why are you saying all these things to me?"

"Because they're true?" But the anger had left her. Maryann hugged a pillow from the couch to her chest and sighed. "I don't know. I feel mean, mad at everything. I can't stand my life."

"It can't be that bad."

"You wouldn't know." Casey could never understand. She lived in a huge house, had a car, had parents who cared even if she whined about them. She didn't know what it was like to live with a drunken slob. It was hard to talk about; it made her feel ashamed. "You don't have a clue."

"Why don't you just refuse to do all that stuff your father makes you do?" Casey asked.

"Yeah, like just say no?"

"If he hits you, report it. Child abuse, right? My mom is on a committee for that."

"Sure."

"Well, it's abuse. It's illegal."

Maryann laughed. "You don't have any idea what you're talking about. Do you know what happens if my father goes to jail? I get put in foster care. It happened to me once when I was a little kid, and believe me, living with him is better than that."

But Maryann was still thinking that she really didn't want to go back. Leaving, going away on her own, it seemed like the only good option. She hadn't figured it all out yet, but she would. "This sucks, you know?" she said, changing the subject. "We can't even make a cup of hot tea."

Casey gave her a crafty smile. "If I'm not mistaken, there's still some wine left."

"Well, it's not like the night can get any worse." Maryann was ready to try to salvage what was left of the night. "Okay, why not?"

If it didn't actually make the girls warmer, at least the wine gave them a buzz. It made them believe Gena was okay and that she'd walk in any minute. If only they had power, they could turn on lights to guide her back to the cabin.

Please don't let her meet up with the police, Maryann kept silently wishing. Give me a break for once and let her come back so we can quit worrying and get on with this stupid vacation and I can figure out what I'm going to do with my life.

"It's getting dark," Casey said.

"It's just because of the storm. It's still early."

"When I was little I used to think I could make a wish come true by counting to five hundred," Casey said.

"So did it work?"

Casey laughed. "I never got there. I'd fall asleep way before five hundred.

"Well, what have we got to lose? Let's count, and when we get to five hundred, maybe Gena will come walking in the door."

Casey shrugged. "Why not? It couldn't hurt!"

The mood had lifted and they couldn't help feeling more hopeful. Or maybe it was just the nice warm glow of the wine. Still, if Maryann said she had seen Gena on the shore, there was a good chance she would come back eventually. They started counting, feeling silly at first and then shouting out the numbers.

They were at two hundred thirty-five when they heard a noise outside. Was it Gena? They didn't dare stop counting, afraid to break the spell. They kept on, two hundred thirty-six, thirty-seven. Finally Casey couldn't control herself; she jumped up and was about to run to the window to peek when there was a knock at the kitchen door.

"She's back! I don't believe it," Maryann shrieked.

Another knock and they both ran to the kitchen. Then Maryann skidded to a stop.

"What?"

"Why is she knocking?"

Casey rolled her eyes. "Because she wants us to open the door?"

"Is it locked?"

The sudden heavy pounding was like a slap in the face. Maryann darted forward and turned the deadlock just as the door started to shake in its frame. The hinges squeaked. A screw came loose and fell to the floor. The door moved a fraction of an inch but the lock held.

They stood there, knowing they should move, but somehow it was hypnotizing, watching as another screw fell, as the wood groaned and buckled. Bang after hollow bang shook the door until, unbelievably, a split appeared down the middle.

Maryann felt Casey clutching her arm. She moved

back, pulling Casey along, watching as the door fell toward them in slow motion, revealing a dark shape behind it. Maryann jerked Casey backward just before the door came down, barely missing them.

They stared, dumbstruck with horror. In the doorway was a nightmare.

The girls scrambled backward, tripping over their feet. There was no place to hide in the kitchen. They backed awkwardly into the living room, and saw that the only option to get away was up the stairs. They ran up fast, using their hands as well as their feet, gasping as they reached the upper hall. There were sounds behind them, driving them on past the bedrooms, until they found themselves at a dead end, looking into the bathroom. Banging into each other, they squeezed through the doorway, shoved the door closed and clawed at the bolt. The small tiled room was a poor excuse for sanctuary.

They stepped into the tub and pulled the shower curtain closed, creating at least a sense of being hidden. Even though she knew it was totally inappropriate, Maryann felt giggles bubbling up inside her—almost a hysteria—from fear and from the hopelessness of their hiding place. They heard a faint thud. Casey slapped her and she froze.

"What kind of animal was that?" Casey whispered.

"No kind I've seen." Except in nightmares, and horror movies, werewolves, the undead, zombies, things that crawled out of a grave. It looked like a person, but it wasn't.

"Did you see his eyes?"

"Who had time?" Maryann replied.

"They were like a person's eyes."

"You mean human?"

"Yeah, only it didn't look human."

"Shit, Casey, a dog's eyes look human too." She stopped and grabbed Casey's hand. "Shhhh. Listen."

Downstairs, cabinets banged open and shut, cans fell off the shelves, bottles shattered.

Maryann allowed herself a small feeling of relief. It hadn't followed them upstairs. Whatever it was had stayed in the kitchen. "Maybe it doesn't care about us. Maybe it just wants food."

They stood there, holding their breath, until finally the noises stopped. Their eyes met. Had it taken the food and gone off? They didn't dare move. They waited behind the shower curtain, straining to hear something that would tell them it was safe: a door slamming, footsteps outside. But the door couldn't bang shut, could it? Maryann thought, not when it was lying flat on the kitchen floor. For several minutes the girls stood in total silence.

"We can't stay here forever," Casey said nervously.

But Maryann had a frightening thought. "What if Gena comes back *now*?"

"If she does, let's pray that thing is already gone. It must be gone. I don't hear anything downstairs anymore."

Maryann was fine with staying behind the shower curtain awhile longer. Forever, if that was what it took. But Casey was pulling the curtain out of the way and getting ready to step out of the tub. And as if this was what it had been waiting for, the sounds started again. Heavy footsteps. Coming up the stairs. A pause as it reached the landing.

Oh God, Maryann thought, clenching her fists so that her nails dug goudges into her palms.

The footsteps came down the hall.

Casey climbed back into the tub, pulling the curtain shut again, shaking.

"Listen to it," she said. "What the heck is that? Humming? It's humming, for fuck's sake."

"Maybe that means it won't hurt us," Maryann said, but she doubted it.

The footsteps stopped. Almost immediately, they could smell it. Right outside the bathroom door.

Images of the mutilated dog, the ravaged corpse raced through Maryann's mind. They were next. If it could tear down a door, what hope was there in a flimsy shower curtain? They were two sitting ducks, waiting to be plucked.

No! the word burned like fire in Maryann's mind. She would fight back. But with what? She looked around at towels, soap, toothbrushes, a couple of wire hangers dangling from the shower-curtain rod.

The doorknob rattled. Casey shrank back into the unyielding tile wall. She whimpered.

"Stay quiet and it won't know we're here," Maryann whispered to Casey, thinking to herself how screwed they were.

The humming stopped. Now they heard snuffling and a low, inquisitive growl.

"Shit, it's going to kill us!" Casey croaked.

"Not me," Maryann said, not caring if it heard her or not. She had too many things she wanted to do. She wasn't planning on dying being one of them.

She grabbed a hanger and started untwisting the wire.

The thing leaned heavily on the door and slowly the wood began to crack.

CHAPTER 26

On his way to meet his father, Ben Jay stopped at Lonnie's house. He'd want to come along, Ben Jay was sure, and they could take his truck. Ben Jay only had his mother's old Mazda, too old to take the ruts up there. And Lonnie sure would want to know that Pope was dead, if he didn't know already.

It took a while for someone to come to the door. It opened a crack and Lonnie looked out, dressed in cut-offs, no shirt. "Ben Jay?"

"You hear about Pope?"

"Only what you said. He's missing, right?"

"He's been murdered."

Lonnie opened the door all the way. He looked terrible.

"What happened to you?" All Ben Jay's worries about a fight came back.

Lonnie shoved his hands into his pockets. "Nothing. Why?"

"You look like shit."

"Partied too hard, I guess."

Ben Jay gave him a long look. "You told me you came home early and went to bed."

Lonnie tensed like a scared rabbit. Said nothing.

"You want to ask me in or am I gonna stand out here?"

Lonnie stepped aside. When he took his hand out of his pocket to shut the door, Ben Jay saw the knuckles. Red, rubbed raw, already black and blue. Lonnie turned away, walked into the family room and sat down. Stared at the blank TV screen.

Silence. Ben Jay waited, then finally broke it. "You gonna tell me?"

"What?"

"You fight Pope?

"You think I killed him?"

"Don't worry, my dad already has a suspect. But you're pretty beat up."

"We had a fight, but it didn't accomplish nothing. He tried to sucker punch me, I let him have it in the nuts. I got a bloody nose, he took a couple of hits. By that time, Norleen was gone. When she wasn't watching no more, Pope lost interest. He wanted to call it off. I never took him for a coward. When I left him near the bait shop, he was walking around on two legs."

"Why'd you go back after him, Lonnie? Haven't you figured out that Norleen *likes* to be with him?"

Lonnie shook his head emphatically. "But she don't. She was yelling at him to get his hands off her. That's why I stepped in." He waited a beat. "So, now he's dead?"

"My dad's pretty sure it's him. The body had that buckle with the skull on it he always wears."

"Must be him."

"You want to come up to see?"

"Naw. I'm gonna hang out here."

Ben Jay was surprised. Lonnie always wanted to go along, no matter where. He hated staying home. That was why Ben Jay hadn't bought that he'd been home watching TV last night.

"You sure about that?"

"I'm sure."

Ben Jay waited, in case he changed his mind. "Okay. See ya."

"Yeah. See ya."

Ben Jay walked back to his car, shaking his head. It just wasn't like Lonnie. Maybe he wanted to stay behind so he could call Norleen. Maybe move in on her now. But still, something was wrong.

CHAPTER 27

The feeble lock finally snapped and the bathroom door caved in. He stood there, massive and bestial, taking up the entire doorway, looking like he touched the ceiling. The skin of his face and arms seemed mottled with dirt until Maryann realized it wasn't dirt but patches of hair, not only on his cheeks and chin but his forehead too, and covering his hands and fingers like thick furry gloves. He had a feral, animal smell that reminded her of the big cat cages in the zoo. Breathing hard, spit bubbles on his lips, he stared at them, humming, grunting, gesturing with his big hands. His fingernails were long and yellow, curling at the ends, like claws, caked underneath with dirt.

He looks like a freaking bear, Maryann thought, but when his eyes met hers they were warm, glistening, intelligent eyes, with knowledge in them, and fear. What did a thing like that have to be afraid of? she wondered. Those eyes almost made her hesitate. Would she be harming a man or a beast? One moment he was looking at her as if he would speak, but in a flash, the humanness she had seen was gone. He lurched forward with a ruthless snarl. Maryann struck.

The sharp end of the uncurled wire hanger went straight into his eye. Maryann was probably more surprised than he was—she hadn't even aimed. There was a moment when he stood there, perplexed, lifting a hairy finger to feel the wire protruding from his face, and then he howled. He snatched at it, yanked it out, and something fleshy slipped down onto his cheek in a viscous fluid. Where his eye had been was a hole filling up with blood. The howling gave way to a terrible whimpering that threatened to tear Maryann's heart. He thrashed around in the small room, falling toward the tub and Casey. Blood spilled onto the white tiles. Whatever pity Maryann felt died as she watched him grab Casey by the hair and lift her up like a doll. Screaming with rage, he shook her, as if she was the cause of his pain. Maryann crouched near the broken door, watching in horror, unable to help.

In a hoarse, choking voice, Casey screamed, "Go! Go . . ."

Maryann knew she couldn't do anything for Casey; she had to find help. She scrambled out of the bathroom on hands and knees, half fell down the stairs and into the kitchen, catching herself before she slipped on the cans of food lying all over the floor. The refrigerator was open, the food they had brought yesterday thrown around. She climbed over the fallen door and stumbled toward the car.

A scream came from the house. Casey was being killed. Gena was probably dead too. I'm the only one left, Maryann thought. Yet in spite of her fear, an idea was forming: Now I can disappear. No one will find me because they won't be looking. They'll think I was killed like the others, my body thrown in the lake, buried in the woods. They can't dig up the entire woods.

She would never have to go home again.

She got to the car, pulled the door open and threw herself into the driver's seat. Get away now! Except she didn't have the car keys. They were back in the house . . . in Casey's purse? On the kitchen table?

She looked at the house. Going back in there was the last thing she wanted to do. She sat frozen, her mind a jumble, until she dredged up the only thing that would give her courage: you have to go back to save yourself, so you can disappear, get a new life. She forced herself to get out of the car, to backtrack to the kitchen door. She stood there a second, listening. Faint thumps but no more screams. With Casey dead, he would come looking for her. She took a deep breath and stepped through the doorway and looked around quickly. On top of the refrigerator was Casey's purse, untouched. Her hands were shaking so much, she could hardly get them to close over the strap to pull it down. She yanked the zipper, got her hand inside to feel for the keys. Found them! She dropped the bag and ran outside. And just like in a bad movie, she dropped the keys. Had to stop and scrape them up from the dirt. At the car, they slipped out of her fingers again. She was crying, her breath ragged as she looked down, tears blurring her vision. Her hand closed over the leather key ring. Got them. She took one backward glance at the cabin to check. Keep moving!

For an instant, everything changed to slow motion: climbing into the seat, holding her hand steady to slip the key into the ignition, reaching out to close the door. Then, with the sound of the door shutting, time returned to normal. She turned the key, stomped on the gas. The engine turning over, the sound of hope. Then hope dying as the engine flooded and died.

Wait it out, don't try to start it again too soon, just count to sixty. She recited the numbers, feeling like she couldn't catch her breath. Her glance slipped sideways toward the house. And there he was, as if by magic, taking up the doorway, somehow blocking the light so that everything seemed dark to her, as if she were going blind with fear. She gasped, tried to breathe slowly. I can't faint. Not now.

She turned the key again. The engine started this time. Blindly, she threw it into gear to back out. The car moved a few feet and the tires sank, spinning uselessly in the mud. The storm had turned the ground into a bog.

She didn't need to look to know he was lumbering toward her. But it was okay, the doors were locked, the windows up. She put the car in drive, desperately willing it to move forward, inch by inch, getting there.

A tremendous thump shook the car and threw her up against the door. Her head hit the window, her arm came down hard and she heard the snap as the lock disengaged. When she looked up, his face was at the glass, staring straight in at her. She could see the pores in his skin, the hairs sprouting from his nose.

"Get away from me!" she screamed, madly fumbling for the lock to push it down again. But he was yanking on the handle and it jammed. She stepped on the gas and the car lurched forward, but he came with it, holding on to the door. With her free hand she grabbed the handle and shoved the door open. He fell hard onto his back, grunting in surprise. "Like that, fucker?" she yelled.

The car continued forward, now on drier ground. She turned the wheel sharply, hoping to aim at him, run him over. But he was standing up again, hugging the car as if he could crush it in his arms. The door still hung open, and he reached in with his clawlike hand and grazed her skin. She scrambled over the gearshift to the passenger seat, shoved that door and tumbled out. She looked back over her shoulder. He had pushed his way into the car and was wedged between the steering wheel and the seat, still reaching for her. Run now, she told herself. But the mud sucked at her feet, slowing her down. Doggedly, she kept going, afraid to take a chance to look over her shoulder. She was getting there, almost reaching the road. I'm gonna make it, she thought.

The smell came first, then the feel of his claws grabbing at the back of her shirt. His ragged breathing was in her ear. He was making a low whining sound. Or maybe it was her.

"Maryaaaaann!"

The shrill scream seemed to pierce her heart, set it pounding faster than it was. For a beat she was confused, and then realized—Casey. Casey was shouting from the cabin doorway, almost unrecognizable, looking as if someone had dumped a can of red paint over her, the blood in her hair, on her face, splashed down her clothes. She shouted again. "Maryann, here! Come on, quick!"

No way am I going back in there, Maryann thought, but his fingers were on her neck and it was only the slickness of her sweaty skin that made them slip. In that instant she felt his strength, more powerful than she could have imagined. There would be no escaping once he caught her. She turned around and ran.

Casey was holding a long metal hook. She reached out with it for Maryann, as if she would catch her and reel her in. Her other arm hung down, the elbow sticking out the wrong way, as if it belonged to someone else. "I know a place to hide," she said as Maryann reached the door. "Upstairs!"

Maryann took the steps two at a time. Behind her, Casey climbed crablike, her body looking all wrong as it twisted its way up.

"You're really hurt," Maryann started to say, but Casey just shook her head and gestured with the hook for her to keep moving. A ladder had been pulled down from the hall ceiling.

"Go up." Casey's voice trembled; she sounded like a very old woman. Maryann went up first, and Casey came behind, struggling with one arm. Maryann helped her climb over the last rung. "Pull the stairs back up," Casey said, handing her the hook.

Maryann snatched at the iron ring at the bottom of the steps. It wasn't easy to pull them up. But the sudden sight of that thing coming down the hall gave her a burst of strength. He stared up as the ladder rose into the air. She saw a last sliver of his face as the door snapped into the ceiling. Casey leaned over and turned a lock.

"My father designed it," she said, slumping down. "One of his jokes. He would hide up here when we thought he was out, then scare us. Sick, huh?"

"Sick or not, I love it right now." Maryann sighed deeply, then paused. "But what if he starts pulling on it?"

"Even if he could reach he couldn't pull the ladder back down. There's nothing to hang on to. It's not like pushing against the old doors downstairs. Trust me, my dad knew what he was doing."

"Let's hope."

The attic smelled of warm wood and dust. They crawled to the far wall, as far away from the trapdoor as possible. There were some cardboard boxes, a faint smell of mothballs.

After they settled down, Maryann had a chance to really look at Casey. There were deep cuts in her scalp and bloody raw patches where her hair had been pulled out by the roots. Her arm was broken and she had welts on her legs, huge purple gashes.

"How did you get away?" Maryann asked, amazed.

"He acted strange," Casey said. "He was yanking me around by my hair, shaking and punching me, and all of a sudden he stopped and looked like he just woke up. I swear, Maryann, he got this sad face, like he was ready to cry. I didn't wait to find out. When he let go, I just ran."

"God, that was lucky. I don't think he felt very sad when he was after me." Maryann shivered at the memory of his claws on her. "What is he, anyway? Did you see all the hair? It's not normal. And did he say anything to you? Do you think he can talk? If it was night and there was a full moon, I'd swear he was a werewolf. It's like he's part animal." Maryann tried to laugh. "But that's really not possible, is it?"

She was babbling. Nervous reaction. Now that they were safe . . . well, relatively safe . . . all the tension just burst out of her.

But Casey hadn't heard a word. She was leaning back against the wall, cradling her bad arm in her lap, actually snoring. Sound asleep.

When Maryann stopped talking, she could hear him in the hallway under them. Snuffling and making that peculiar humming sound. How long would they have to stay up there before he went away? *Would* he go away?

CHAPTER 28

A stairway to heaven. Two angels ascending. The thought pleased him. It was like the way he would think about things *before*.

The two angels got away. Clever. Fooled him, and that was something new. They had escaped for now, but he would get them back. They were unfinished business. His father had warned him: never leave a thing undone.

He looked up at the ceiling where the ladder had gone up. His view was strange and lopsided. It seemed too flat, with some kind of fog of red over everything. Gingerly, he touched his eye and his finger came away wet and dark. The pain had been very bad but now it was gone. His head felt numb, as if he'd been to the dentist for an injection. He thought about going to the bathroom to look at the eye in the mirror. Just an idea, he knew he wouldn't do it. He never looked at himself. If you didn't look, you could be like the picture you had of yourself in your mind.

He sat down on the floor in the hallway. He had many things to do, but right now he was tired. He'd take a short rest and then go back to the secret place where the other one was waiting. The food, he reminded himself, don't forget the food. All this trouble had been caused by food. But without food, people starved, and when people starved long enough, they died. That was something he knew about. He'd learned that on his own, without his father having to teach him.

CHAPTER 29

She felt cold. Wet. I was in the water, she remembered. I didn't drown. Images in her mind were shadowy and vague. She moved her leg and pain shot from her hip to her ankle. Something was wrong with her shoulder. How did I get here?

Where *was* here?

It was dark and damp. Sitting on dirt. She must be in the woods. Maybe she could make it to the cabin. If only she could see. This blackness was wrong. If she looked too long in one spot, ebony turned to bronze to mottled purple, and quicksilver explosions went off in the corners. Then everything shimmered, clouded and went back to black again. There were shapes too, growing into huge goblins, into figures moving toward her, then away. What was real and what wasn't?

"Is anyone here?"

Her voice was scary in that black void. Why had she been left there alone?

Then she remembered. Fear punched her stomach and took her breath away. The world had turned upside down and she had been lifted and carried, a journey without time. Hours? Only moments? It hadn't been a dream.

The air smelled closed up and musty. Above her the black was unyielding and starless. She reached out, hesitantly, and touched nothing. Lifted her arms above her head and felt nothing. Forced herself to crawl in spite of the pain and kept reaching. Each inch she managed brought relief. She was not in a grave. Maybe it was a cave. A cave was better; it meant she had not been buried alive.

Then a new fear came. What if there was a ledge, a pit? She would have to feel the ground with her hands, to make sure she didn't reach an edge. Her heart skipped. Up to now she had been intent on exploring the boundaries. Now she thought of what might be here with her. Snakes. They would slither silently. If only there were just a sliver of light.

And then her hands went to her face, her fingers moving across her eyes. What if I'm blind?

With the panic came the undulations of the darkness, black upon black, swirling shapes, the hint of faces. She no longer could tell the difference between what she might be seeing and what she imagined. The worst of all was the thought that someone could be there, near her, watching her, and she wouldn't know.

The scream erupted from her against her will. She screamed until she was hoarse, all the while a part of her knowing how useless it was. Make me stop, make me stop, she thought. She started coughing. Her throat was dry and sore, and when the last echoes of the screams faded from her ears, the silence was deafening.

Then into the silence came a small sound. A weak sound, like a bleat. An animal, not human.

Another cry. Was it saying "help"? Or was it her imagination? Had hoping too much created a hallucination?

But then the words became unmistakable. "Somebody? Help? Please?"

She moved her head, trying to pick up the direction, the way a cat does, or a dog, pricking their ears and turning their heads, tuning in. She didn't feel afraid. If the voice asked for help, it must have been someone like her, trapped here, put here against his will, not someone who would hurt her.

"Somebody?" the voice came again.

"Yes! I'm here! But where are you? I can't see."

"Oh god, thank god, over here."

She moved forward and her head struck something hard. The blow made a noise in her ears that ran through her body like an electric shock. A wall. She felt it. Cold stone.

"Keep talking! I'll find you."

No answer. Just silence. Was this a joke? Was she blind and someone was teasing her, getting a laugh as the blind girl crawled around on her hands and knees in a perfectly lighted room?

No, she had to believe and hope. She would follow the wall now, let it guide her.

The opening was as unexpected as the wall had been. Her hands reached into space and she fell forward onto her face. For a second of terror she thought she had reached the edge of the chasm she had envisioned earlier, but then she realized it was a doorway. Another room.

There were more smells now, urine and feces. "Where are you? Talk to me so I can find you!"

"Somebody here?" the voice asked.

"Yes. I'm trying to find you. It's dark. It's really dark, isn't it?" She bit her lip, dreading the answer.

"Dark as a sonofabitch."

Thank God. She could forget being watched. No one could see anything here.

"Keep talking."

"Hard to talk. Wait. I'll sing. What do you like, country, rock? The fourth caller will win a prize." Strangled-sounding laughter followed.

All her suspicions came back. Someone playing with her like a cat with a mouse. Or maybe worse. She was locked in here with a crazy person.

"Who are you?" she asked. "How long have you been here?"

There was a choking sound. "I'm just hanging around. . . ."

"Look! This isn't a joke!"

"You got that right."

It must be a crazy. She'd be safer if she didn't get near him. Better just sit still, say nothing.

After a while: "You still here?"

She didn't answer.

"Hello? My name is Jeffrey Wayne Kimble. My Social Security number is two four—"

"Jeff? Is it you?"

"Yeah?"

"We were looking for you, searching in the woods— where'd you go? They said you went for a walk and—"

"Who are *you*?

"Gena. Casey's friend. We went to see Lane this morning and he said you were—"

"Casey! She's here?" Jeff sounded confused. He paused as if he was trying to think, get his bearings. "Lane didn't think she meant it."

"We came with her, Maryann Blethen and me. Lane said you went for a walk. Why didn't you go back? How did you get here?"

He gave a grunt. "Probably the same way you did."

"I don't even remember. All I know is something weird happened."

"You didn't see him? Count yourself lucky."

Hearing from Jeff that it was a he, a person, made Gena feel frightened in a way she hadn't up to now. Not knowing had been scary, but this was scarier. An identity meant a real threat. Someone who had a purpose. Who wanted to kill them.

"Are you tied up?" she asked, wondering why the same thing hadn't been done to her.

That creepy laugh again. "I'm hung up! And that's not the worst thing."

Hung up? Tied up? Gena wasn't sure what he meant. And what was the worst thing? She wasn't sure she wanted to know but couldn't stop herself from asking. "What?"

"He has teeth and he bites. But not just that. It's like . . . he's eating me."

Gena almost physically pushed this idea away, moving back a little. "Come on, is it an animal? How could an animal tie you up?"

"Not an animal. He talks. But he's not human either."

"Are you sure about this, that he's . . . biting you?"

"Yeah, I'm sure! When somebody takes a chunk out of your leg, you know it."

None of this could be true. It had to be a joke, Gena thought, and she almost felt better. It was some kind of cruel game. Who was playing it? Lane? Casey? Was it some elaborate hoax, and when she came through it they'd say she passed the test?

"Okay. Okay. That's all. I'm not doing this anymore," she said.

"What? Do you think I'm making this up? You've got to try to get out of here, get help. Or you'll end up like me."

Gena was quiet for a minute. "Jeff, are you serious?"

"Come over here," he insisted. "If you can smell me, you can find me."

Maybe this was the final test, the last step. Whatever it was, she would find out for sure. She stood up slowly. The pain shot through her leg, as bad as a toothache. She swayed, losing her balance in the dark with nothing to guide her. She walked forward, hands out, while Jeff said, "Keep coming, I'm here, here." And then she walked into a pair of legs. Swinging.

"Omigod."

"I'm sure I stink really bad by now. Being tied up like this, you know, I had to pee in my pants." He giggled, sounding crazy. "Can you smell the blood? I'm the dinner here."

She didn't want to touch him. But she believed now. Because she could smell the oniony smell of stale sweat, and the metallic odor of blood.

She slipped back down and sat on the floor.

"Gena? You there? You gotta find a way out. There must be a door because he gets in here. Find the door."

"I can't. I can't see. I don't know where I am."

"Try, okay? Just give it a shot."

She was lost in the middle of nothing. She couldn't

even feel a wall anymore. She would walk around and around and get nowhere.

"I can't."

"You've got to! You want him to string you up like this, like a side of beef? Who knows what he'll do to you . . . a girl."

"What do you mean?"

"What do you think I mean?"

I can't I can't. Her mind wanted to shut down. She felt sleepy. She just wanted to go home.

"Gena!" When she didn't respond, he called her name again and again.

"Okay, fine!" she finally yelled back. "I'll try."

She turned away from him and began to crawl once more, one hand outstretched, into a sea of darkness.

She felt as if she had crawled over the dirt floor for miles before she found the wall again. But there was no way of knowing which wall. Still, it was like she'd found some long-lost friend, she wanted to hug it.

Jeff's voice kept on at her at intervals. "Where are you now? . . . Did you find it? . . . Keep going."

She was tired and dirty and sore. But she kept going. And then her hand touched something other than the cold stone of the walls. Wood. A step. A ladder!

"I found it," she said. Then louder. "I found it! Jeff, I found it!"

She sat there, breathing deeply, feeling a spark of hope in her triumph. She didn't realize she had been looking upward, as if anticipating climbing into freedom. The sudden light hit her eyes like an atomic blast. White light as bright as sun off new snow struck her with agonizing pain. Her eyes instinctively squeezed shut but the burning went on and on. If she had thought the dark was blinding, she knew the light was much worse.

Then suddenly the light was blocked with a dark shape. It was coming down. She could smell it, feel it, hear it humming in time with the buzzing in her head.

There was no more dark anymore. Eyes closed or open, she could see only luminous torches burning an afterimage of a nightmare. Whatever it was had returned.

CHAPTER 30

B en Jay's car couldn't make it to where the body had been found. The track leading up to the spot was nothing but mud after the storm, and his old tires were about bare. He pulled over to where Delbert was lounging against his cruiser at the bottom of the track. Delbert and his brother Dexter were the sheriff's two deputies. They were twins but they looked nothing like each other. Dexter was good-natured and sort of looked like a monkey. He had the habit of pulling down his upper lip to hide his oversized teeth. His brother Delbert got the looks in the family. People called him pretty boy, but he could be meaner than catshit. Seeing Ben Jay arrive, he gave him a long look. "What you doing here, boy?"

"Wanted to see what's going on. Is it Pope?"

Delbert nodded. "Went and got hisself killed."

"How did it happen?"

Delbert raised an eyebrow. "Your diddy know you snooping around *po*lice business?"

"Sure. He told me to come up here to meet him." Ben Jay realized he was getting better at lying, what with all the stories he'd had to tell recently. He looked up into the woods, where he could see the lights of the cruiser spinning through the trees. "Only I don't think I can drive my car through that mud."

Delbert nodded. "That was a real gully-warsher we had."

"You see the body?"

"Yup. Tore up bad."

It was like pulling teeth, Ben Jay thought. "How bad?"

Delbert treated him to a suspicious squint. "What you want to know for?"

"Just wondered if it could have been an animal. My dad says there might be a bear around here. Tore up some animals yesterday, at one of the old cabins."

"I heard about that. Coulda been a bear attacked Pope. But I ain't seen no bears around here in years. You?"

"No. Lonnie and I go camping here all the time, and we never ran into one."

This got Delbert laughing. "You don't want to be running into no bears."

"Who's this suspect you got down at the jail?"

"Better ask your diddy that question."

"Come on, Del." Too bad I don't smoke, Ben Jay thought. Delbert likes mooching a smoke. Get him talking.

"Some drifter who don't belong here," Delbert relented. "Looks like a bad gadget too. All tore up hisself. Been in a fight, that's for sure."

"What did he say about it?"

"Dee-nied it." Delbert snorted. "Says some critter attacked him."

"Maybe it did. What if it was the same thing that got Pope? And the same thing that tore up those animals in the cabin?"

Delbert shrugged. "First I gotta see the bear."

"You know anything about animals being killed in the north, in Tennessee? I heard something on the news about it. Some cattle on farms, a horse. You guys heard about it?"

"I ain't heard nothing like that."

"Think anybody else might?" Ben Jay was determined to get something out of the deputy if he couldn't actually see the body.

"You asking a lot of questions, boy."

"I'm just curious."

Delbert laughed snidely. "You know what they say, key-uriosity killed the cat."

Ben Jay backed off. If he said too much, Delbert would make some joke of it and spread the word around, and then his father wouldn't pay any attention to Megan McCauley when she came.

There was movement up in the woods and the cruiser's lights came down toward them. The police van followed. The body would be in a black body bag inside. Ben Jay wished he could see it, but he knew his father wouldn't open the bag now. There had to be a way to sneak a look, though. He needed details to compare with what Megan McCauley knew and what he had seen in the cabin.

The sheriff rolled down his window. "Good thing you didn't try to get up there in that mud," he said to Ben Jay. He nodded to Delbert. "That's about it."

Ben Jay waited until the deputy got back in his car and left before he asked, "So do you think that dude you arrested did it?"

"Easy enough to find out. There was blood all over his clothes. We get it tested and see if it's the same type as Pope. If it is, we'll get the Georgia Bureau of Investigation to do a DNA test to clinch it for sure."

Blood test. Ben Jay thought about Lonnie's knuckles. He didn't believe Lonnie had anything to do with the dead animals he found in that cabin. But Pope was another story. Lonnie had straight up admitted he fought Pope. What if he hit him a little too hard? And what if, seeing that Pope was dead, he made it look like an animal did it, like the bear his father thought was responsible for the massacre? It would be a clever way to cover up the crime. Question was, was Lonnie that clever? Would he actually mess up Pope when he was dead to steer suspicion in a different direction? A person would have to have an iron stomach to tear up a body, and he didn't think Lonnie was the type. But who knew? Lonnie following Norleen, *that* was something Ben Jay wouldn't have suspected.

One question just seemed to lead to another. Like Delbert said: too many questions. He'd have to wait to hear the results of the blood tests. If Pope's blood type matched the blood of the guy the sheriff had arrested, that would be the end of it. Although not necessarily *the end* of it. There was definitely something going on in these woods. Something very strange. Ben Jay hoped that he and Megan McCauley would be able to figure it out.

CHAPTER 31

In any ordinary small-town police facility in Georgia, it would have taken a while to get blood analyzed. It would have had to be sent to Atlanta, where it could take days, maybe even weeks to be processed. A town the size of Delonga wasn't exactly a priority. But lucky for Delonga, the sheriff's department had Doc Valentine. The doc's hobby was forensics, and he had a special lab set up in the back of his veterinary office. There had been times when he'd identified some parasite or diagnosed a disease in time to save someone's pet. That was where the blood samples taken from Billy Pope's body and the clothes taken off Trash Macey had gone, and before six o'clock the same day, they had the results.

It was no use pretending the sheriff wasn't disappointed. In fact, he was downright pissed off. Billy Pope, of all people, the ornery lowlife that he was—and even the sheriff had to acknowledge this, although it was speaking ill of the dead—turned out to have the rarest type of blood in the world, type B. What made him deserve such distinction the sheriff could not imagine. Life would have been much easier if Pope's blood had matched the blood on the perp's clothes. But no, the perp had the most common blood type, type O, and there was absolutely zero crossover. Samples from the perp's bloodied clothes bore no traces of type B, just as Pope's body bore no traces of type O. From all indications, the boy in the cell was innocent.

"You're free to go," Dexter told Macey, holding the cell door open. Trash looked at him like he was crazy.

"I'm naked, here," he said.

Dexter came back with some clothes for him to wear, not Macey's own bloodstained and torn rags but somebody else's cast-off jeans and shirt. Trash dutifully dressed, not wanting to spend another second in the jail. The jeans were too big around the waist, but Dexter gave him his belt back. The shirt wasn't one he would have chosen, but beggars couldn't be choosers. He was just glad the clothes were clean and he could get out of there.

They gave him back his wallet, which had miraculously survived, but there was nothing else. Pocket change, watch, cell phone, cigarettes and lighter were gone. He looked in the wallet. A five and six ones. He had money stashed in the truck, but there was still the problem of keys.

"Is there a garage in town I can call? My truck is out

there in the woods. I lost the keys." No sense reiterating the story of the attack. He figured they still wouldn't believe him.

"Closed on Sundays," the deputy said. "But they'll come out tomorrow morning and give you a tow."

"Thanks, but what do I do in the meantime?"

The deputy gave a long look back toward the cells, then shook his head. "Try the motel out by the highway. Tell them Dexter said to give you a room. Half price. It won't come to nothing. Rooms ain't very expensive to begin with."

Trash was going to ask how he could get to the motel without a ride, but he decided it was best to leave before that sheriff got back and thought of something else to pin on him.

"Thanks," he told Dexter, and turned to leave.

"You take care," the deputy said.

You bet, Trash thought. If he ever got back home, he planned to take care for the rest of his life. He hurried out onto the street. Sunday evening. The town looked dead. The diner was closed. There was a bar down near the road to the lake if he remembered right. But going in there, even for just a burger, was probably asking for trouble in a town like this. The sheriff would give him a Breathalyzer for drinking a Coke.

Luckily, it was still light. The only plan he could think of was to find his way back to his truck and sack out in that cabin again until morning. At least he knew the cabin had a couch. Far as the motel went, it was nice that he got a police discount, but he had no idea where it was or if he could even walk there. He had a better chance of finding the cabin again—and, he hoped, his truck.

He remembered that he'd driven around the lake until the first fork and then had taken the road with the big loblolly pine. The next fork he thought he might recognize too. If he could get that far, maybe things would look familiar enough to find the cabin.

The funny thing was, he wasn't even thinking about the girls anymore. They were out of his mind completely. He found the fork and the pine and it gave him a spurt of energy. He was feeling pretty good considering he was beat up, had no socks and hadn't eaten since the deputy had given him a cup of coffee and a dry cheese sandwich that morning. Trash had a feeling it might have been the guy's own lunch. Looked homemade. He kept walking because he had nothing else to do and he wanted to find the cabin before it got dark. If he didn't, he'd be lost and it would be last night all over again.

He hurried. He hoped he'd taken the right fork the second time. Nothing really looked familiar, but then all these trees looked the same anyway, so how could he tell? He was hustling along when he saw something out of the corner of his eye. He almost walked right past. When he stopped and backed up, he saw a red car. *The* red car. He was at the girls' cabin again.

He stopped and looked closer. The car was the right one, but it looked a lot different from when he'd seen it before. Both doors were open, the one on the driver's side hanging half off. The windshield had been smashed, which made Trash immediately think of his own truck. His windshield smashed, their windshield smashed. How much of a coincidence was that? There was something wrong here.

Hadn't he been looking right into this cabin, watching one of the girls prancing around, and the next thing he was waking up in his own grave? Whatever it was, it had gotten him right here in this spot. And who was to say it wasn't still hanging around?

Aware that he was exposed there out in the open, he stepped off the road into the bushes. Things seemed quiet. But things had seemed quiet last night, and look what had happened to him.

He peered around, checking it all out. He saw that the side door was wide open and what looked like a piece of floor was jutting out. There were canned goods on the steps, like they'd rolled out the door.

Trash was torn. Should he take a closer look? Or should he mind his own business? Maybe whatever had happened, they must have already called the police. What he didn't need was to run into cops again. Pinning this on him would be a piece of cake! But there were no cars in sight and no radios crackling. Everything was quiet. The place had a creepy look about it, like it had been abandoned. Like whatever bad thing had taken place was over, and everyone had gotten the hell out.

He stood in the bushes, thinking, staring at the

canned goods. That was something he could definitely use. Food. There would be no food back where his truck was. No hope of a meal until tomorrow.

It was tempting, but the thought that maybe there was a dead body or two or three inside made him hesitate. If he went in there, left traces of himself—he'd heard a lot about how you couldn't help dropping a few hairs or spit even if you were super careful—the sheriff would get him again. He'd be a sitting duck.

But he was hungry. He'd take one quick look inside. If he saw bodies, he'd haul ass. If not, he'd take a can or two. And figure out how to open them when the time came.

He kept to the bushes as he inched toward the door. At the last moment, he sprinted out to the steps, careful to avoid the cans. A broken leg was the last thing he needed. Inside the kitchen, he knew something big had happened. The door wasn't open, it was lying there, off its hinges, in the middle of the kitchen floor. There was a mess all around, food, cans, stuff from the fridge. But no bodies.

Trash was curious. What had happened to mess the place up like this? Must have been one hell of a party. He decided that before he got the food, he'd take a look around. If nothing else, maybe he'd find some smokes. He crept along, trying not to make a sound, watching out for hazards.

He peered into what looked to be the living room.

What do you know? His lucky day! A pack of cigarettes on the table. He would just step in, grab them and be on his way.

And that was what he did. Got the pack, turned around. And looked right into the eyes of a ghost.

He screamed. The ghost screamed.

Trash stumbled backward, thinking this was how people got heart attacks.

CHAPTER 32

B en Jay realized there was no stopping his father. The sheriff was going to talk to Lonnie.

"I can't treat him any different from anybody else, Ben Jay," his dad insisted. "I'd question anyone who was seen near the lake last night. I know you're thinking I think he's guilty, but what if he saw something that will help us catch the SOB that did this?"

Ben Jay had to concede that it made sense, but he still couldn't help saying, "Lonnie had nothing to do with Pope dying." That was what he hoped, at least, that Lonnie hadn't hit him too hard or walked away without checking whether Pope was hurt bad.

"If he had nothing to do with it, then he has nothing to worry about."

There was no way Ben Jay couldn't be worried. Once his father saw Lonnie's raw knuckles and the remnants of his bloody nose, he'd know something went down. Those blood tests Doc Valentine was so good at would show for sure that there was some kind of connection. One way or the other, Lonnie would be in deep shit.

Ben Jay was in the cruiser with his dad, going along to Lonnie's house. His dad could be informal like that, let him come along on a case. Of course, until now, any suspects his dad questioned were people he thought had kicked in the soda machine at the garage or had stolen somebody's hubcaps.

"Let me ask you something. Why are you so het up about Lonnie?"

"Dad! He's my friend."

"I know that. But there's something else going on here. You're nervous as a cat. You know something you're not telling me?"

"No, sir."

His father gave him a long look. "Okay then. We go and have a word with him, find out why he was in such a rush to get out of my way last night; he explains and it's cleared up. Then we ask him if he seen anything suspicious when he came back."

"Yes, sir," Ben Jay said, and then gave a start. "Came back?"

"You wouldn't know something about that, would you?"

"Uh . . . no, sir." Ben Jay was confused. What did his dad mean about coming back?

His father looked at him doubtfully. "You think your

old man is as useless as a sore thumb?" He gave a laugh. "That's what that dog woman said to me. She lost her cool, as you'd say. Didn't sound so priss proper when she was cussing me out for not finding her little Biscuit."

"He's still missing?" That didn't sound good. Sure, the poodle could be lost. Or chewed up like those other animals. But he wasn't gonna tell his father about his suspicions yet. He hadn't told him about Megan McCauley coming down tomorrow either. He'd decided to let her explain. Coming from her, it would sound more real.

Ben Jay was nervous all the way to Lonnie's. He hoped his friend could explain things better than he had earlier that afternoon. His father wouldn't buy that *came home, watched TV, went to bed early* routine. Lonnie would have to tell the truth.

Normally, parents would be able to tell the sheriff whether their son was home at night. But Lonnie came and went through his bedroom window more often than not, to avoid his mother, who could be cranky or hot tempered in the evenings after she'd had her "medicine," which everyone knew was vodka and water. His father would be in his bed where he always was ever since his stroke. What Lonnie needed was an alibi. Ben Jay sure hoped he had a real one.

When they got to Lonnie's house, Ben Jay realized why his father had let him come along. He was the decoy. He thought about turning around and leaving, but then just figured he'd just get it over with. If his dad didn't talk to Lonnie now, he'd send Dexter or Delbert out to bring him to the station. Resigned, Ben Jay walked up to the door and knocked. "Hey, Lonnie, it's me."

When he opened the door and saw the sheriff standing behind Ben Jay, Lonnie shot him a dirty look.

"There was nothing I could do about it," Ben Jay mumbled as they went inside.

Mrs. Crane was in the kitchen sitting at the table. She gave the sheriff a dirty look herself. "What you want, Hayworth?"

"How you doin', Miz Crane? Just want to talk to Lonnie. Nothing serious now, just get some things straightened out."

"My Lonnie didn't do nothing."

"I didn't say he did." The sheriff turned to Lonnie, who was slouching in the kitchen doorway. "Take a load off, boy," he said. "Sit down here with your mama."

Ben Jay knew his father had to question Lonnie with his mother there, since Lonnie was still a minor. He also knew his dad would have preferred it if Mrs. Crane could have been in another room. She tried to answer every question his father asked before Lonnie could open his mouth. But it soon became clear that she couldn't account for Lonnie's movements the night before, or explain his bruised knuckles.

"Miz Crane," the sheriff said patiently. "It would be a lot better for all of us if you could let your boy answer for hisself. He's old enough to know what he did or didn't do. You let him talk and things will go a lot faster and we'll be out of your hair."

"Don't go preaching to me, Hayworth."

"No, ma'am. But we have to get this over with." He looked at Lonnie. "So you want to tell me what's what?"

Lonnie looked from the sheriff to Ben Jay. "He told me about Pope," he said, nodding to Ben Jay. "I had nothing to do with it, okay? Yeah, I admit, we had a fight. But no way did I hit him hard enough. When he saw . . ." Lonnie stopped.

When he didn't say anything else, the sheriff prodded, "This have something to do with Norleen?" Ben Jay was surprised his dad knew about Lonnie liking Norleen.

Lonnie looked away.

"Son, if you're innocent, you got to tell the truth. You don't say anything, it can only look bad for you. You know that."

Abruptly, Mrs. Crane got up from the table. "I'm calling Fred Barston," she said huffily.

Fred was a lawyer in town who'd handled wills and deeds for what seemed like a hundred years. He had to be eighty or ninety, Ben Jay thought, and not much help when it came to crime. But Fred Barston was probably the only lawyer's name Lonnie's mother knew.

"Ma! Forget it," Lonnie burst out. "Okay. It was about Norleen. Like I already told Ben Jay." Lonnie threw him a look of gratitude for not repeating it to his father. "Pope was bothering her when I ran into them, talking to her like a dog. I told him leave her alone. He bowed up and said, 'What are you gonna do about it, beat my ass?' I said yeah, if that's what it took. He laughed and told me to forget it. Started walking away like he wasn't gonna fight. I figured fine, if that's what he wants to do, and then he turns around and sucker punches me." Lonnie rubbed his jaw where a bruise was beginning to show. "He swung first."

"Okay, Lonnie," the sheriff said. "What happened after that?"

"We fought. It ended. Pope was as alive as you and me when I left."

The sheriff took in Lonnie's skinny arms, his small stature. Pope had at least thirty pounds on Lonnie and was known as a dirty fighter. "So you won?"

Lonnie's face took on a deeper shade of red. "Naw, I wouldn't have stood a chance, but when Pope saw Norleen was leaving, he went after her. She gave him the finger, told him she wasn't going to see him no more. Then he was madder at her than me. He started yelling after her, looked like he couldn't believe she would do that."

"That was the end of it?"

"Well I figured after Norleen was gone he would turn on me again. So I got in my truck fast."

"And did Pope go after Norleen?"

"No, sir."

"Is that right? He let her walk off, didn't do nothing about it?"

"Yes, sir."

"I find that hard to believe," the sheriff said.

What was his father insinuating? Ben Jay wondered. Did he think Norleen killed Pope? Then, looking at Lonnie's red face, he thought he knew what might have happened. But he had to let Lonnie tell it. If Lonnie could ever get it out.

"He told you what happened," Mrs. Crane fussed. "Leave him alone now. You always were snaky, Hayworth."

"Yes, ma'am," the sheriff said to her. "But I'm not trying to accuse your son of something he didn't do. Just want to get to the truth."

Lonnie looked like he was going to burst like a ripe tomato. Ben Jay tried to urge him with his eyes. "Come on, Lonnie," he whispered.

"I . . . ," Lonnie said, gasping out the words, avoiding his mother's eyes. "I was with Norleen. I picked her up on the road and drove her back."

"And did she invite you in?"

Lonnie nodded.

"What time did you leave her house?"

Lonnie croaked. "I spent the night."

Mrs. Crane rounded on him. "You what? With that white trash?" She was ready to launch herself into a tirade, but the sheriff stopped her.

"Norleen will vouch for that?" he asked.

Lonnie looked miserable. "I guess so."

"Okay, Lonnie. That's it for now. Thank you, Miz Crane."

Mrs. Crane scowled and Lonnie seemed to deflate, folding himself into one of the kitchen chairs.

On the drive over to Norleen's, Ben Jay started to feel better about his friend. It looked like Lonnie was hiding a few things, but they weren't at all what Ben Jay had been worried about. And once Megan arrived, he'd have bigger things to worry about.

Their second visit of the day didn't start out as successfully as the first. When they knocked on Norleen's door, she opened it, took one look at the sheriff, cursed him out and slammed the door in their faces. His father got ready to beat on the door again but Ben Jay stopped him.

"Let me. I'll talk to her. It'll be better if I do."

He told his dad to drive away so she could see he wasn't with him, and when the cruiser was gone, he knocked again. Norleen stuck her head out, her face hardware glinting.

"I gotta talk to you. It's important," he told her. "Otherwise, Lonnie's going to be arrested for killing Pope."

Norleen laughed. "As if."

"Please?"

She looked like she was thinking of saying no, then relented.

She spilled the whole story, the same as Lonnie's. He had indeed spent most of the night with her. "This is gonna give Lonnie a reputation," she added, and laughed.

Ben Jay had a feeling Lonnie might not mind.

When the sheriff heard that Norleen had agreed to back Lonnie's story, even to sign a statement, he frowned. Not because he disapproved but because he was right back where he started from, without a clue to who killed Pope, without a suspect. Which meant whoever *had* killed him was still out there.

It was hard to believe that only yesterday the sheriff had been complaining that nothing exciting ever happened in Delonga. "Be careful what you wish for, son," he said to Ben Jay.

CHAPTER 33

They asked the same question at the same time. "What happened to you?"

"I got attacked. . . ."

"This monster . . ."

Their stories came tumbling out, incoherent, on the edge of crazy, too fast to take in. They both had to take a breath, calm down. Each spoke with a sense of horror and disbelief.

But Trash felt relieved. Not only did someone believe him, but some of the same things had happened to them both. "It's gotta be the same guy."

"If it *is* a guy," Maryann said. "He looked like he was part animal."

Trash thought about it. "He's human enough to know how to destroy a vehicle. Like he didn't want either of us being able to leave. That takes some kind of reason."

"And that's exactly what we have to do. Get the hell out of here before he comes back. Only . . ." Maryann raised her eyes to the ceiling. "Casey's up there and she's really hurt. She won't be able to walk."

Trash thought for a second. "You got a phone?" There was no way he could keep away from the cops now. But maybe this time, when they saw the evidence, when Maryann backed him up and told what had happened to her, they'd be sorry they didn't take him seriously. If they had listened to him, they coulda maybe caught the guy.

But Maryann was shaking her head. "Casey had a cell and it's gone. I guess that's another thing that makes him human. He knew to take the phone."

Trash nodded. "He took mine too."

"There's a phone here in the house, but it's not turned on. Nobody knew we would be here." Maryann was visibly at her breaking point. "What are we gonna do?"

Trash looked around. By now it was dark inside and out. That thing could be hanging around the cabin, or out on the road, in the woods, waiting. No way they could walk back to town in the dark, especially not carrying Casey. But if they left her here?

"We need to wait until it's light; we can't go out in the dark." Even in the light there was the possibility of meeting up with that monster. "Where is she?"

"Up in the attic. She's unconscious. I couldn't carry her down. We hid up there, that's the way we escaped. It seemed like I waited forever. When I couldn't stand it any longer I had to risk coming down. He was gone, thank god. When I heard you, you came this close."—she held up two fingers with a minuscule space between them—"to getting your head bashed in." When she'd come down the stairs, Maryann had had a fireplace poker raised above her head, ready to strike. "Do you think you could carry her down here?"

"Yeah, guess I could." An unfamiliar feeling went through Trash, something he had never experienced before. He felt, what? Good about something? What could be good about this mess? Still, it was there. A nice feeling. She was counting on him to help.

"Sure, I'll do it. Show me where it is."

Maryann led him upstairs. There was a bad smell in the hallway. "That's from him," she said. "He really stunk." Yeah, Trash thought. He recalled something like that.

A ladder was pulled down from the ceiling. Underneath, in a big circle, the hall runner was torn up in patches.

"He did that," Maryann said. "He sat here waiting for us, ripping it to shreds with his claws, hoping we'd come down so he could get us again. Did you see his long nails? He used them on Casey to tear out her hair." She shuddered.

They climbed up the steps. Casey was in the corner, slumped against the wall. Trash was scared when he saw her. Her skin was white as a sheet, and her head was all bloody. She was making a strange sound as she breathed.

"She looks real bad," he said. The thought of leaving her there left his mind. She'd die for sure, although he didn't know what they could do to prevent that even if they stayed with her.

"She's alive," Maryann said anxiously, like she wasn't convinced herself. "That's good, right? It means she's fighting. We need to keep her alive until we can get help."

Trash had never carried someone like that before, and down such narrow steps. But to his complete surprise, he was able to do it. He put her body over his shoulder. She was dead weight—like a two-hundred-pound guy even though she was so skinny—but he managed. Somehow he knew to turn around and back down the steps. Like a firefighter, he thought. He must have learned it from the movies.

When they finally got her downstairs and put her on the couch, she was moaning. Her eyes fluttered open, but all Trash could see was the whites.

"What do we do?" Maryann asked. Again, expecting him to know.

"Get some blankets, keep her warm." That's what you were supposed to do with people in shock, right? "Put her legs up on the couch arm. Keeps the blood from leaving her head, or something. She feels real cold." Like a dead body already, he thought.

Maryann did what he said, like he was a doctor giving orders. He thought maybe it would be good to wipe some of the blood off her face, out of her hair. Jesus, there were big ugly wounds where the hair had come out.

He cringed thinking about how it must have felt. "Maybe we should put something on those," he suggested.

"Good idea. I'm sure there's something in the medicine cabinet upstairs." She ran up without thinking, then stopped cold when she came to the bathroom door, which was hanging off one hinge, splintered down the middle. The room still smelled of him. The shower curtain had been pulled off its hooks. There was blood in the bathtub, on the floor and in the sink. Some of it was his. She crept over the floor, feeling sick that she might touch something that came out of him. In her head, she could hear Casey's screams.

She found peroxide and cotton and a tube of antibacterial ointment in the cabinet. It was probably a good idea to clean the sores so they wouldn't get infected, but peroxide would really hurt. She was afraid to give Casey any more shocks. She grabbed the ointment instead.

When she got back to the living room, Trash was staring down at Casey, looking really concerned. Maryann had always thought of Trash as some redneck to stay away from, but now she didn't know what she would have done without him.

Casey didn't seem to feel anything at all when they put the ointment on her head. After they covered her up, Trash said they should start a fire. With the kitchen door torn off, it was growing damp and cold in the cabin. Trash went to try to prop the door up. Both of them were thinking the same thing: the gaping hole was an invitation for *it* to come in. Doors hadn't done much to stop him before, Maryann thought, but somehow she'd feel better if the doorway was at least covered.

Scavenging around, she found newspaper and more wood and lit the fire. It smoked a lot at first, and Casey made some bad sounds in her throat. But then the flames were burning bright and the smoke was going straight up the chimney.

"I hate to ask this," Trash said, coming back from the kitchen. "But do you have anything to eat?"

"Sure, yes." Mary Ann realized she was hungry too. When had they last eaten? It seemed a very long time ago, when things were normal.

They opened a can of soup. Since there was no power, they poured it into a pot and set it next to the fire. There was half a loaf of the bread left from their peanut butter sandwiches yesterday. Somehow it had escaped being torn up or thrown around like everything else. The butter from the open fridge was soft, which was fine. They sat on the floor in front of the fire, sipping soup and eating bread and butter. If it hadn't been for Casey lying on the couch, and the constant sense of being alert, for fear of that thing coming back, it could have been like a picnic.

"Is that really your name?" she asked, breaking the silence. Somehow, with everything that had happened, she couldn't bring herself to address him as Trash.

He shook his head.

"Well, what is it?"

He seemed reluctant to tell her.

"Come on, it can't be that bad. What is it?"

"Same as my father's name," he said, and she caught a nuance in his words.

She felt sorry that she'd pushed him. From the tone of his voice, it sounded as if the name had bad connotations for him. She wouldn't want to have *her* father's name. "It's okay, you don't have to tell me if you don't want to."

"I don't tell most people."

"Never mind."

"It's Eustis," he blurted out.

"Uh . . . well, that's not so bad." Looking at his face, she started laughing. "I'm sorry. It's just . . ."

"After my father, Eustis Raeford Macey. He was a real asshole."

Then Trash was laughing too, and for just that second, they forgot. Until a sound came from the couch, a long, painful moan.

They stopped laughing.

"Sorry, Case," Maryann whispered.

In the flickering light of the fire, Trash felt for her hand, closed his own over it and held tight.

CHAPTER 34

After the brief blinding light, it was dark again. Gena didn't dare move. She tried not to breathe, wishing she could dissolve into the blackness. But he knew she was there.

Suddenly the light was in her face.

She couldn't help herself: she scrabbled away over the dirt floor. "Get away from me!"

"Why are you afraid?"

The voice was nothing like she had imagined. It sounded perfectly ordinary. She heard no taunt or threat behind the question. If anything, it sounded puzzled.

Gena would have liked to reply, but so many reasons welled up inside her, disordered, angry, confused, that when she opened her mouth, she couldn't speak.

"Cat got your tongue?" he asked, and now there was definitely a taunt, a teasing tone.

Anger came to the surface, giving her false courage. "What do you want?"

"That's better," he said. As abruptly as it had been turned on, the light was extinguished, making the dark worse than before. "Are you hungry?"

The question took her completely by surprise. It was mundane, but it scared her. What purpose did he have in feeding her? She remembered Jeff saying he was being eaten. I'm dinner, Jeff had said grotesquely. Her heart kept skipping beats. The thought of food was revolting.

"I brought you something," he said.

There was a rustling of paper and then something was thrust into her face. It smelled familiar. Ham? Ham and cheese. Was he going to make her a ham and cheese sandwich? She almost laughed but stifled it so that only a choked gurgle came out.

"Yes, you sound hungry."

"I'm not hungry."

"Sure? No? Too late!" She heard the smack of lips, chewing. He was eating.

"Turn the light on again."

He didn't answer. Minutes ticked by and she was sure he wouldn't do it. Then she saw a bright shaft of yellow reaching upward. He was holding a flashlight aimed at the ceiling.

An instant, then it was gone.

"Wait!"

"Say please."

The word choked her but she forced herself to say it.

The light was precious, more important than food, more important than anything right now. "Please."

The light appeared again, moving in circles, reaching up to the fathomless dark.

"Say thank you."

"Thank you."

"You're welcome."

She couldn't see him, just a hulk in shadows. She didn't want to see him. But not seeing made her mind come up with horrible pictures of what he could be like. Which was worse? Knowing or not knowing?

She heard him moving and the shaft of light wavered, then righted itself. It became her anchor. It made her feel real, not like a faceless shadow.

Then Jeff started yelling. She didn't want to think of what might be happening. He had moved away from her, silently, leaving the light. Could he see in the dark? What *was* he?

Slowly, cautiously, she crawled toward the flashlight. With it she could find the ladder and the door.

Maybe it was a trap, but she didn't care, she just wanted to get her hands on the light. Moving toward it, trying to be as quiet as possible, her hand came down on something hard. And familiar. My god! A cell phone. She felt it, snapped it open. The bluish glow of the dial was like the best thing she had ever seen in her life.

She had just dialed 911 when something struck her arm. So hard, so much pain, she could feel it in her teeth, in her brain. She screamed and groaned, she could hear herself begging. She couldn't shut herself up.

Her chance was gone. She touched her arm. Surely it was broken. She was afraid to feel the skin, to feel a bone sticking through. The pain encompassed her. Nothing mattered anymore. The pain was eating her alive.

"Bad girl," he said, his voice so close, a growl, nothing ordinary about it. "This calls for punishment!" He crowed it, as if this idea made him the happiest creature in the world.

Gena felt herself fading into another place where she could hear nothing but a smooth lapping of what sounded like the ocean. Sorry, Mom, she thought. Then her thoughts became a swirl of color as red as blood and she was gone.

PART THREE

Monday

CHAPTER 35

When Maryann woke up, Trash's arm was around her. They had talked for a long time, discovering that they had a lot in common, especially their families, their fathers. Maryann found herself talking about things she had never told anyone else. She even told him about what she wanted to do, how she had planned to disappear and not go back home, until the thing, the man, whatever it was, attacked the car and prevented her from getting away.

They kept checking on Casey. Maryann was afraid if she didn't keep a constant watch, Casey would fade away, die when nobody was looking. As it was, she was deathly pale and hardly breathing.

It got late and they were tired, but neither one of them wanted to fall asleep. Both of them were still on the alert, even when they seemed relaxed, listening to every sound, getting up to check the windows. When Maryann had to use the bathroom, she made Trash come up with her and stand at the head of the staircase. Before, hurrying to get stuff for Casey's wounds, she had been able to go up there alone. But now there was no way she could go anywhere by herself. She felt awkward without a bathroom door, but he turned his head. She looked at her face in the mirror, saw how haunted her eyes looked. She scrubbed off the blood she was surprised to find on her skin, wondering whose it was.

"We have to try to get some sleep," Trash said. "We'll take turns. One of us will keep watch. You go first."

It was a good plan but Maryann kept jerking awake, thinking that thing was in the room, standing over her with his claws. She told Trash to go ahead and take a nap, but he also tossed and turned. Finally, when there was the faintest glimmer of dawn, they both lay down in front of the glowing embers of the fire. A moment before she fell asleep she felt his arm go around her, and it made her feel safe for the first time since she and Casey had heard that thing pounding on the kitchen door.

It seemed like only minutes later when she opened her eyes and then realized she'd been awakened by a noise. Trash was awake too.

"What?"

"Somebody's outside," she whispered.

They sat frozen, listening. Voices. But instead of welcoming the fact that someone had come to help them, they were trying to pretend they weren't there at all.

"Yo!" a voice called out. "Casey, Gena, Maryann! You in there?"

"Who's that?" Trash asked.

Maryann leapt up from the tangle of blankets. "It's them. The guys we saw yesterday. Casey's boyfriend, Lane. Thank god!"

Trash didn't feel quite as excited to be rescued by Casey's boyfriend. Probably some college boys. For a while he had actually felt like *somebody*.

But when Maryann came in with them, he saw they were just ordinary guys like him. He recognized the one with the long blond hair—the one supposed to be Casey's boyfriend. He'd seen him around, but he didn't know the other guy.

Trash could tell they were shocked when they saw Casey lying on the couch. Lane looked like he was going to faint. "What the hell happened here?"

Maryann and Trash tried to explain, but the two guys kept interrupting and asking questions.

"Look, we don't know any more than what we're telling you," Trash said.

Bailey looked around the room. "Where's Gena?"

"She's missing," Trash answered.

"Did you find Jeff?" Maryann asked.

And it all started falling into place. The mangled dog. Jeff and Gena gone. Casey and Maryann attacked. "And it got to you too?" Bailey asked Trash. "Jeez, what kind of animal *is* it?"

"It's not an animal," Trash tried to explain again.

"Like we told you, it's too intelligent. It walks around just like a man, and it knows about trucks and cell phones."

"What does he want?" Lane thought out loud.

"He's a killing machine, that's all I can guess," Trash said.

Maryann was suddenly frantic. "Look, we're just wasting time. You've got to get Casey to a hospital. She has to go right now!"

"Okay," Bailey said. "Let's get all of you out of here."

Maryann shook her head. "I'm not going. You just take Casey and get her to a doctor fast."

Bailey looked startled by her words. "You can't stay here. He might come back."

"Never mind me. Take her now and go! Look at her, she's dying!"

Bailey hesitated, wanting to talk her out of staying, but Maryann wasn't changing her mind. At the hospital everyone would ask questions, including the cops. No way was she going to get involved with all that. Her idea of pretending to be dead wouldn't work now, but she still had a chance to take off. With all the excitement, it would be a while before they'd start searching for her.

Shaking his head with concern, Bailey went to lift Casey off the couch. Lane said to Trash, "You coming?"

Trash hesitated. He thought about facing the sheriff again, maybe even the state police, what with Casey so badly injured. Forget that. "I'm staying with her."

"You're both crazy," Bailey said. "Come on, Lane, let's get out of here. She's barely hanging on."

As the two boys carefully carried Casey out of the house, Maryann and Trash looked on. Maryann was scared. She looked at Trash. "You sure about this?"

"I'm sure."

Her heart settled down. "Okay. I'm glad. But I have no idea what we actually do now."

With the boys gone, Trash felt decisive again. "We go back to my truck. You help me pry the hood up and I wire it. Then we find that garage the deputy told me about, get the windshield replaced, and we're out of here."

Maryann smiled. They'd put miles between them and this nightmare of a town. Maybe Trash would help her disappear. They'd figure it out.

"Sounds good to me," she said.

CHAPTER 36

B en Jay and his father were having breakfast. The
sheriff was distracted, thinking about Billy Pope's
death and the next step in the investigation. Ben Jay was
nervous, thinking about Megan McCauley's arrival. He
had tried to reach her yesterday evening; he'd left a message to fill her in on Pope. He hoped his father would
push off soon so he'd be home alone when she arrived.
That way he could talk to her privately and they could
share their theories. He could also warn her that his father was unlikely to be sympathetic to them.

The sound of a car pulling up at the house interrupted the silence, and his father got up to look out the
window, anxious to see if it was Dexter or Delbert coming with new evidence to nab the murderer.

"There's a woman out there," he said.

Unfortunately, it looked like Megan McCauley was early.

The sheriff opened the door before Ben Jay could get it. A young woman stood there.

"Is this where I'll find Ben Jay Holcomb?" she asked.

The sheriff looked her over. "And who might you be?"

She put out her hand. "Hi, I'm Megan McCauley, with the *North Georgia Star*? Ben Jay's expecting me."

"I'm the sheriff," his dad said, stepping back so she could enter the house. "Ben Jay's my son." He gave Ben Jay an inquiring look. "Were you expecting company?"

"Right, Dad, I invited her to come. She has some information for us that might help. With the massa— murders." Megan McCauley was a lot younger and prettier than he had expected.

"Well then, come on in," the sheriff said heartily, and Ben Jay knew he was being razzed. "Sit yourself down. As you can see, we're just finishing up breakfast. Coffee?"

"Thanks," Megan said. She put out her hand to Ben Jay. "And you must be he."

"He? Oh yeah, Ben Jay. Hi."

She sat down at the kitchen table, laying her briefcase at her feet. Ben Jay sat across from her, feeling awkward, while his dad poured a mug of coffee.

"Sugar, cream?"

"Black, thanks."

The sheriff sat down and looked at them both.

"Better fill me in. Ben Jay hasn't had time to let me know what you two have been talking about."

Ben Jay felt a big sigh of relief. At least his dad wasn't going to make him look like an idiot.

"We've been discussing the possibility of a connection between some animal mutilations in the North with those Ben Jay told me about here in Delonga. Now I hear you have a human body that's been badly mutilated as well."

"Is that a fact?" His dad glanced over at Ben Jay. "Well, yes, the body of a boy was found, badly tore up. We've already eliminated a couple of suspects, although I haven't put them completely out of the picture."

This was news to Ben Jay, who had figured Lonnie was in the clear. He didn't know anything much about the other guy they'd pulled in except that he thought he'd been cleared too.

"Human victims are a new development," Megan said. "There haven't been any human bodies along the trail from Tennessee, just mutilated animals. But there was one homicide in Juniper, where I believe this all started."

The sheriff cocked an eyebrow. Ben Jay realized he should have warned his father, told him at least something about all this. But then, would he have paid attention? Right now he could be humoring them.

"Maybe you better start from the beginning," his dad told Megan.

She explained about the fire in Juniper, and the incidents that occurred before it. A house owned by a family called Penny, a mother, a father and a son named Wayne.

Ben Jay left the table momentarily to collect the pages he'd printed from the Internet, as well as the other information about the animal mutilations. When he brought them back he could see that his father had been listening intently, but Ben Jay couldn't tell what he was thinking. He handed the pages over and the sheriff gave them a glance.

"The problem is," Megan said, "we don't have any concrete evidence to link all this together. We don't even know if the boy, or man, as I suppose he is now, was in the house at the time of the fire. His whereabouts are unknown, although I did talk to someone at the hospital where he was treated for a few years and I learned a lot that was very disturbing. But there isn't one specific fact or piece of evidence that could be the key."

The key. Ben Jay had all but forgotten about the key.

"What kind of house was it, where the fire was?" he asked.

"Very old Victorian type of place. Didn't look as if anything had been done to improve it in years and years."

"Well, I fail to see—" his father began, but Ben Jay jumped up.

"Wait!" He ran to his bedroom, and when he came back he opened his hand to reveal the old-fashioned key he'd found at the cabin where the animal massacre had taken place. "Would a key like this possibly work in that house?"

Megan and the sheriff looked it over. "Where'd this come from, son?" his father asked.

"The cabin where the animals were. Lonnie and I went back there to take a look. I found this outside the back window. It looked as if something had escaped that way. Maybe heard Lonnie's truck and climbed out. You could tell by the bushes that something heavy had dropped down from the window."

His father was looking at him in astonishment. Megan was turning the key over and over in her hand.

"The closet," she said. "The old man was locked in a closet after he was killed. This might just be the key that fits that lock. If the boy was in a hurry, he might have put it in his pocket without thinking, before he ran."

It sounded good to Ben Jay. "What do you think, Dad?"

"It's a nice theory, folks. But that's all it is. A key is a key, it can't talk and it doesn't give me anything to go on. I fail to see how this relates to Billy Pope's death."

"It could be the same guy, Dad!" Ben Jay said. "He laid a trail of dead animals from that town, Juniper, to Delonga. When he killed those animals in the cabin and jumped out the window, he dropped the key."

"And he suddenly switches from animals to Billy Pope?" The sheriff was skeptical. He turned to Megan. "Do you have a description of this man you're talking about?"

"I don't know what he looks like now, but I do have some odd facts about him. It seems he suffered from a medical condition know as hypertrichosis. It's sometimes found in feral children, and it may be a factor in the belief in wolfmen or werewolves. It can be caused by a number of things, malnutrition being one, and—"

"Hold on!" the sheriff said. "What does all that mean in plain English?"

"He was very hairy."

The sheriff laughed. "Well, if that makes a man a murderer, I better worry about some of the fellas here in town. I know a few have a lot of hair."

"With all due respect, sir, this isn't normal body hair. Hypertrichosis means hair growing where it usually doesn't grow, like on the palms of the hands, the soles of the feet, the forehead, nose and ears."

The sheriff frowned now. "And these so-called feral children. This man is one of those?"

"Not really. There are records of kids being found in the wild, supposedly living with animals, who were covered with body hair. But it eventually disappeared when they got back to civilization. This man was raised with his parents. He spent some time in a state mental facility, where they noted the hypertrichosis. But he never lived in the wild, as far as I know."

"He's living in the wild now," Ben Jay said excitedly. "He's been wandering all the way from Tennessee, and nobody's seen him. And if he killed the animals in the cabin, he's living right here in Delonga, in the woods."

The sheriff didn't like this theory at all. It didn't fit in with his idea of what a murder investigation should be. He still didn't see the connection between a bunch of dead animals and Pope. And who was this girl? A reporter. Lord knew, they liked to stir shit up. Write a story about aliens or some hairy wolfman, you sell a lot of newspapers. He gave Megan McCauley a doubtful look.

His cell phone rang.

"Excuse me a minute." He got up from the table and went into the other room.

Megan turned to Ben Jay. "Your father is a hard man to convince."

Ben Jay nodded. "He likes things to be . . . normal. He didn't listen when I said it was weird for all those animals to be killed together in that cabin."

They could hear the sheriff talking. His voice was suddenly strident, giving orders.

He came bustling back in. "Got to go now. Those boys who found Billy Pope? Now they've brought a girl to the hospital."

"Who is she?" Ben Jay asked, thinking of Norleen.

"Nobody from around here. And they're talking about another girl who's missing. Seems a bunch of them have been staying in one of the cabins. I tell you, there's something mighty suspicious about those boys. Delbert's holding them at the hospital. Nice to meet you, Miz McCauley, and hear your story, but I need to be on my way."

"There's more to it, I'm afraid," Megan said.

"Well, I'm sorry, but I just don't have the time right now. Don't know when I'll be back, son." And with that he ran out to his cruiser and drove off, siren wailing.

"I have a feeling this is all connected," Ben Jay said. "The animals, Pope, the girls. Everything has happened in the woods around the lake."

Megan nodded. "Is there any more coffee?"

When Ben Jay had filled her mug, she said, "Sit down. I'm sorry I didn't have time to tell this to your father. I hope you've got a strong stomach, because this gets pretty bad."

CHAPTER 37

Megan launched into her story immediately. "This man, Mr. Penny—the poor old guy who was killed and left in the closet before the fire? It all begins with him. Everybody I talked to on Hopecrest Street described him and his wife as a sweet old couple. They were recluses but wouldn't hurt a flea, the usual stuff. It seems like neighbors are always describing a murderer as the nicest guy in the world."

"Right. Like Ted Bundy," Ben Jay said. "Everyone trusted him, thought he was perfect."

"Until the very end, when he started acting strange. But yeah, that's what I'm talking about. Somehow these psychopaths manage to live a completely double life."

"That's what Mr. Penny did?"

"I'll bet my bottom dollar on it. Everything I've been

able to dig up points to the fact that poor old innocent Mr. Penny was a predatory serial killer."

"And this is the father of the guy who's been killing animals?"

Megan nodded. "And the father may have not only been killing but also eating his victims."

The thought made Ben Jay gag.

"We don't know if Wayne Penny did the same to this Billy Pope, but it looks as if he had been attacking and mutilating animals. Eating animal meat isn't cannibalism, of course—though eating it raw isn't common, or normal, for that matter. But cannibalism is often part of a predator's profile," Megan explained. "You've heard of the famous ones, since you're up on all this. Jeffrey Dahmer was one who made the news. But there are lots of them in the files. Gives them some kind of power."

"So they don't eat because they're hungry?"

"It's a ritual. And there's evidence that this is what Mr. Penny did. The equipment in the basement, for example. Forensic tests showed that the big pots had contained human flesh and fat. The iron rings on the walls? That's where he hung his victims up. God knows what he did to them."

"And his son was in on all this?"

"That's the really terrible part. It isn't bad enough that the old man was a killer. It looks like he used Wayne as a decoy. My theory is that he took him along in the car and offered these women a ride. They went missing from places where they might have been stranded, or were hitchhiking. It's an easy way to find victims. And what could be a better lure than a young boy in the car? Even if the women were suspicious at first, they'd see a man with his son and feel safe accepting a ride."

"That's . . ." Ben Jay searched for the right word.

"Diabolical," Megan finished for him.

"But wait. If the kid was hairy, like you said, wouldn't it freak them out—the women? He'd look too weird and scary."

"It's possible his father removed the hair, shaved it from his face and hands. That would be easy enough. And the women were probably picked up at night, in the dark, so they wouldn't look too closely. The boy may have been instructed to act a part, play with toys, be friendly."

"Why would the kid do it?"

Megan shook her head. "Why not? It was his father. And maybe he didn't really know the whole truth about what his father did with them. Though as he got older, it would have been hard to hide."

"And what about the mother? Don't tell me she went along with it also?"

"I don't know. I couldn't question her about it. She was found outside the kitchen door. Wayne might have made sure she was safe. That could indicate she wasn't part of it, that he didn't want to punish her the way he punished the old man."

"But if he *was* in on it, why would he kill his father?"

"Probably because he had been forced to do what he did. Wayne was a victim himself. When he got old enough to fight back, he did."

"But if we're right, he's still doing it, isn't he?"

"Think about it. It was *women* his father wanted. There were the stories about animals being killed, people's pets, but the father must have focused on women. I think Wayne was kept as a prisoner in that house. Now that he's free, he kills only animals. We don't know about this boy Pope that was killed, although it sounds as if the body was mutilated the same way. But the kid could have got in Wayne's way, or threatened him. It could have been self-defense, not an intentional killing."

"But there are also those girls, the one in the hospital and the one who's missing."

"That could be unrelated, like your father said. What's the story on the boys who reported it? It sounds to me like a party gone wrong. Bunch of them come up here to a cabin for the weekend and it gets out of hand? We have to wait to hear what the injuries are."

Ben Jay thought about all the reading he'd done on serial killers. Demented, every one of them. He'd never expected he would actually find one on his own doorstep. It was interesting as a theory, something to read about in a book. But now the possibility that it was happening for real, right here in Delonga, made him physically sick.

He thought about what he'd read about cannibalism. The real cases, not the ones in the movies like *Hannibal* or *The Texas Chainsaw Massacre*. In fairy tales, witches always wanted to cook up kids for a meal. You could laugh at that. But when it was real life, it was pretty awful. There was a famous case, Albert Fish in New York. He even sent a letter to the mother of one of his victims, saying how tasty her daughter was.

"So what do we do?" he asked Megan. "You think we could find this Wayne Penny? I don't think my father is going to take it too seriously."

"That's a pretty tall order for just the two of us, Ben Jay. This man is dangerous, even if he is confused and sick. Let's say he *did* kill Billy Pope, and maybe attacked the girls, the one in the hospital and the one who's missing. I'm not sure we'd have much of a chance."

"But to just sit here, while my dad is off on the wrong track . . ."

"If we put the facts together and make a strong case, he'll have to listen."

"You don't know my dad."

As it turned out, the sheriff was a believer within an hour. He phoned Ben Jay and told him to lock up the house, keep Megan inside and make sure he was on the alert.

"What's going on, Dad?"

"That hairy business she told us about? Seems there's something to it after all. The girl here in the hospital, she was almost a goner. Before she passed out, she was able to describe what she thought was half man, half animal. Came into their cabin and attacked her and her friend." There was urgency in his father's voice. "You keep these details under your hat, hear? I don't want a panic spreading. We're getting a search party together. Another girl is missing since yesterday. Those idiot boys never said a word. Trying to protect the girls, they said. Seems they're runaways. But now we've got word about some 911 call coming from a cell phone. They're trying to do a trace."

Ben Jay tried to absorb all this. "Dad! The search party? I'm going too. I'll call Lonnie. You've gotta be convinced he's not involved now, right?"

"Yeah, I am. But I want you boys to stay put."

"We know those woods better'n anybody."

He heard his father's hesitation in the way he was breathing. His dad was excited. This was the biggest thing that had ever happened here.

"All right. You get Lonnie and y'all come down to the station. But you tell that reporter woman to stay in the house or take herself back to where she came from. I don't want this turning into one of them media circuses."

"We'll be there right away, Dad."

"Oh, and Ben Jay? Looks like that missing dog's been found. Biscuit? I'll have to break the news to the owners. Those boys have some kind of nose for finding dead bodies. I'm not sure I have the whole story on them."

"You don't think they did all this?"

The sheriff just snorted. But before he hung up he added, "Candy-ass city boys."

Ben Jay told Megan what had happened.

"He believes you. I'm just sorry it took this to convince him."

"You think that girl in the hospital will be all right?" Megan was still businesslike, but Ben Jay could tell she was affected.

"I guess so." Ben Jay answered, distracted. He could hardly worry about that now, with the other girl still missing. "I'm gonna have to leave."

Megan put down her mug. "Where are you going?"

"They're organizing a search party. Me and my friend Lonnie will be in it."

"I'll get some things from my car, change my shoes." Megan stood up to run out to her car, but Ben Jay grabbed her arm to stop her.

"Uh. My dad says you need to stay here."

Megan gave him a look. "You're kidding, right? This is why I came all the way down here. No way are you leaving me behind."

CHAPTER 38

"Eat," the thing said, pushing Gena's head forward. She recoiled from the swamp smell of rotting flesh as he tried to force her face into Jeff's bloody arm. She felt her teeth click against bone. His salty blood was on her lips, making her gag.

She twisted away. "Are you crazy? He's a person! I know him!"

Jeff wasn't speaking. Maybe he was unconscious. She hoped he was.

She felt the rough earth under her as she was dragged back into the other room.

"You won't eat the food I brought before. You won't eat meat like me. You'll starve." He sounded angry and impatient.

Gena was horrified. She was crying and shaking, she couldn't control it, but that didn't stop her from choking out an answer. "Don't worry, I plan to be out of here be-fore I start losing weight."

"If you don't eat meat, you starve. I know that for an actual fact," he said.

"Okay, sure, it's a fact, you can starve if you don't eat," she said, like she was talking to a child. "But it doesn't happen so fast. I can go a few days without eating meat. For god's sake, vegetarians never eat meat and they don't starve!"

Why was she even explaining this to him? He was insane.

"I don't understand," he said. And he sounded genuinely confused.

"Okay, I'll tell you again. You can eat all kinds of things besides meat. Vegetables, fruit, bread, spaghetti, pizza. You must know all this."

"My father said to eat meat. It's good for you. So you won't starve. You need meat. The meat of life. Must have it. Good for you." His voice rattled on, repeating the words like a litany. She wondered if he really knew what he was saying.

"You're a cannibal," she said.

"What's that?"

"Someone who eats human flesh. It's wrong."

"It's wrong." The statement came out flat. Like he didn't understand what *wrong* meant.

There was a long silence, and she hoped he would leave her alone now. But she could tell he was still nearby. He hadn't turned on the light for a long time.

She was convinced that he could see in the dark. Everything pointed to him being an animal except for the fact that he could talk, reason and ask questions. He asked a lot of questions. She welcomed that at first. If she kept him talking, he couldn't do anything to her. She'd heard that was a good thing to do, make your captor talk to you. But it tired her out. And after all the talk, what happened? He wanted her to take a bite out of Jeff's arm. It was totally insane. It was worse than any nightmare. With a bad dream, you had an option—you could wake up. No matter how she had tried, there was no waking up for her here. If only she could be back home, back before she had ever agreed to come on this trip with Casey and Maryann. Where were they, anyway? Why hadn't they come looking for her?

"It wasn't wrong before," he said suddenly.

"What?"

"Before now. With my father. Not wrong then, he didn't say so."

"I don't really know what you're talking about." And I couldn't care less, she thought. She wanted to go to sleep and forget. "Leave me alone."

She'd had to suffer all kinds of indignities. Having to pee like crazy and not being able to hold it in—they never showed you stuff like that in movies. Nobody ever had to go to the bathroom in a horror movie. They could be down in a crypt forever and never have a twinge. Though now, since he hadn't given her anything to drink, she wouldn't have to worry. She'd probably die of dehydration.

Nobody would even know where she was. That suddenly seemed like the saddest thing in the world.

"Maybe you can tell me some things," he said.

Sure, she thought. Tell him how her whole life was being ruined? Tell him how it felt to think about being dead? But then again, it was talk. So long as he was talking to her, he couldn't do anything else. "What do you want to know?"

"It's wrong to eat flesh?"

Oh all right. She'd humor him. She had nothing else to do. "I told you. It all depends on what flesh you're talking about. You can cook steak, you know, from cows? Chicken, beef, lamb, pork—oh, and fish. People eat that and I guess it's technically flesh. But it's from animals and you eat it cooked. You buy that kind of meat in a store, you understand?"

"We cooked it sometimes."

What was he talking about? "Yeah, that's good."

"But it was flesh."

"That's right, cooked meat is okay. But it has to be meat you buy. Animal meat. You don't eat people. You certainly don't kill them so you can eat them. Do you understand that? It's wrong. You need to let Jeff go. Get him to a doctor."

She heard the weird humming he did. Sometimes it sounded like just singing to himself. Now it sounded like angry bees.

"No," he said finally. "It's all right to eat a person,"

He hadn't heard a thing she'd said. Gena screamed "No! It's not all right! I told you."

"If your father tells you to do something, then it's right."

Oh my god. This was really insane now. She gave a sarcastic laugh. "If your father told you to eat people, it was definitely wrong."

"My father was wrong?" he asked. But she was not going to be sucked in. You couldn't reason with a crazy person. Let him rant away. She was keeping quiet now. He kept talking.

"Down in the cellar it was very dark. All the time. I had to stay down there with them. The bodies. Sometimes they cried. They asked me to help. Let me go. Let me go. I didn't do it."

She didn't want to hear this. She hoped he was making it up, a fantasy. A crazy person's delusion.

"That was wrong?"

She didn't answer.

"You say that was wrong?" he yelled in her face. So close. She hadn't realized.

"Yes, yes, it was wrong."

"You must obey your father."

"Not if he makes you do something bad."

He started roaring. She could hear him moving around, away from her, screaming at the walls in the dark. Roaring and then sobbing. She began to think that something terrible had happened to him. He sounded so pitiful that against all her better judgment she heard herself asking, "Are you okay?"

"I was wrong. Maybe yes. But I did the right thing. I killed him."

Omigod. "Who?"

"Him. She was going to tell on him. She said enough is enough and it was all over and this is the end. He smacked her and made her cry. She said 'Let me go, let me go,' sounding just like the bodies. I had to hit him. He fell down. I took him to the cellar to the place where he kept me. I put him in the bin."

"The bin?"

"Where he kept me. I locked the door, took away the key. But she cried. Scared. Told me they would find out."

"Who cried?"

"Her. My mother. He was hitting her, so I hit him."

What could she say? She was afraid to speak in case she set him off again.

"Nobody will know. I burned him up. I did the right thing."

He seemed to want her agreement. "Yes. You did the right thing."

"Good."

"Yes, good."

"Now I will bring you food. The right kind of food. Not flesh."

"Thanks," she said weakly. Did this mean he was going out? She might have a chance to get out the door.

"I will give you the light," he said. "I know you want the light. Not like me, in the dark all the time."

She felt the flashlight being put into her hand and she could hardly believe it. A feeling came over her, like being grateful, like she wanted to thank him over and over, forgive him, tell him it was all right, tell him she wanted to help him. It sounded like something really bad had happened to him. She felt sorry. Maybe it wasn't his fault.

She turned the switch. The beam of light shot out into the darkness.

And she saw him.

Something out of a nightmare. Her worst dreams and fears, a demon, a wolf, a thing covered with black hair, with one red burning eye and sharp teeth. She screamed and turned the light off.

But in that instant, she had also seen something else. It barely registered when she was looking at the specter in front of her, but now that she was in darkness, it blazed in her mind like a thousand-watt bulb. A cell phone. Undamaged. Not the one he'd smashed. This one looked perfect, lying almost in front of her. All she had to do was put out her hand.

He was growling in anger. She had done the wrong thing, screaming. He knew she didn't like what she had seen.

A new fear washed over her like cold water. It was in the air, in the earth beneath her, in her mouth and in her heart. How had she ever believed he would let her go?

And then, from a long way off, she heard voices. The sound of dogs barking.

She could tell he was listening. He heard it too.

"We all die here together now," he said in a new voice, one like steel, like the sharp edge of death.

She grabbed for the phone, turned her back on him to hide the light, punched in the numbers. She didn't know if she made a connection. She was screaming then. "I'm here, I'm down here, help me!"

Then she felt his hand close over hers and the phone was wrenched from her grasp. She fell back to the dirty ground, her will seeping away. I'm going to die, she thought, and it was as if she didn't care, it was all a mistake and she shouldn't have talked to him, she should have taken the flashlight and used it as a weapon. She had been wrong to feel sorry; never feel sorry for your enemy, she would remember that.

Suddenly something was lifting her up. Above her a small speck of light was opening into a circle, an explosion of brilliance. She wasn't dead, she heard voices and she could feel arms around her, his arms. They were climbing up into the light. It was him. Unbelievably, he was carrying her out. Her eyes teared, twinged with pain, and she could not look.

"It's okay now," he said in her ear, and she could smell his rank breath and feel the heat of it.

"It's okay now," someone said again, but this breath was minty and fresh.

She felt them around her, people. Something cool was placed over her eyes. Then there was a sharp intake of breath, as if everyone there had gasped at once and she knew he had come into the open and they had seen the horror of him.

CHAPTER 39

It was hard for them to understand that it was a man. This was something they would talk about for years afterward, how they unearthed a monster from the old plantation cellar, a long-forgotten place that had once been part of the Underground Railroad, helping slaves to reach freedom.

To Ben Jay, who knew better, Wayne Penny hardly looked human. He was broad and powerful, his limbs like the trunks of trees, his skin like bark, and covered with straight black, soft-looking hair. All over. Cheeks, nose, forehead, ears. Down his arms and covering his hands. Whatever clothes he had worn were half rotted away and the hair was everywhere. One eye had been injured and was closed, a crusty slit. The other eye was black and flinty, sharp and darting. Bushy eyebrows merged above them. He stood in the center of the circle that had formed. He snarled and exposed long yellow teeth.

Wolfman indeed, Megan thought. If there had been others like him, this was certainly how the tales got started. She knew he had been born to Mr. and Mrs. Penny, it was in the records. He had come to the state hospital as a young boy, not half as frightening as he was now.

There were men who were raising the rifles and shotguns they had brought along, the guns they used for hunting possum and squirrel in these woods, aimed now at this half man, half beast. He didn't deserve to die here on the spot, without mercy, without a trial. The sheriff barked orders for them to stand down.

But Wayne Penny gnashed his teeth and lowered his head like a bull about to charge. To Ben Jay he looked more confused and scared than menacing, but the men weren't seeing that. They didn't know what this was in front of them. All they knew was that it looked inhuman and dangerous. They hadn't noticed that he had brought the girl out to them.

When they had found the camouflaged old door in the earth and lifted it up, they'd seen the monster's face first, looking up at them like a caged animal. The rifles had been aimed then, ready to fire, in spite of the sheriff's shouts. But then they had seen the girl and they backed off. The monster had lifted her and climbed up the stairs, then placed her gently on the ground.

Gena had been taken to one of the trucks, a wet cloth over her eyes. But she could hear the sounds of agitated men. She took the cloth away and saw what was about to happen.

"Don't hurt him!" she cried out, but it was in a feeble voice. No one heard. No one paid attention.

He looked like an animal standing there, cocking his head like a dog would, panting and drooling, and the crowd lost another degree of sympathy.

Megan inched forward, blocked by the circle of men with their guns. "Let me through."

"Get back there, little lady," someone said. "Let us handle this."

"Give him a chance," Megan said. "You don't understand. . . ." It was unconscionable that they would execute him in cold blood. No matter what he had done, he deserved a chance to have his say. But the men were edging her out, and she realized there was little she could do.

Wayne Penny stood silently in the center of the circle of men, as if weighing the odds. There was something in his look, intelligence, suffering, a fierce determination. Megan saw it. Ben Jay saw it. But abruptly it went out, like a light turned off, a fire snuffed. His unhurt eye went dead. He had given up.

Only a few realized or suspected that what he did

next, he did on purpose. Knowing there was no escape, knowing that death was really the only way out, he sprang forward as if to attack.

"Nail the critter," someone said.

The guns went off, explosion after explosion, enough to kill ten of him.

"Got the bastard."

He stumbled, amazingly still alive, took a few steps and looked at them before he fell. The noisy crowd went quiet. The sheriff began cursing. People started talking, excited, wound up.

"He asked for it." "Nothing else you could do." "What choice did we have, him coming at us like that?"

Gena watched from the truck, tears running down her face. Maybe death was the only choice, she thought. Part of her hated him, appalled by what he had done to Jeff. But seeing him lying there, just a broken body, it all seemed pointless.

"Are you okay?" a woman asked.

Gena looked up.

"I'm Megan," she said. "I know you're upset. I don't mean just because of what you went through. You got to know him, didn't you? Something made you realize he was more than an animal.

"He was human," Gena said.

Megan nodded. "His name was Wayne Penny. He was born human like everyone else. But someone else turned him into what you saw. It took guts to survive down there in that hole with him. It's not your fault he was shot."

Ten yards away, Ben Jay stood looking down at the body. How had it been to live like that? Nobody would treat him as anything but an animal. So he became one.

"It's over, folks," he heard his father saying. "Everybody go home."

Epilogue

The summer sun beat down and baked the earth dry. Casey sat on the terrace, turning brown everywhere except for the scars on her arms. They stayed pristine white, like coiled snakes, matching the twisted dreams inside her head. The head that was covered by a wig.

"Nobody will know it's not your own hair, dear," her mother had said.

Casey was scared all the time. It felt like eyes were watching her no matter where she was. She didn't go to school or see friends; she never went anywhere. Her mother told her Lane had asked about her at the country club, but Casey had no feeling at all. Lane was from another life; he didn't mean a thing.

Except for an hour every day spent sitting in the sunlight, which her mother insisted she do to get vitamin D, she stayed inside, curtains drawn, doors locked. She didn't believe that animal thing was dead. It would come back. And when it did, she wouldn't be able to do anything about it.

Trash talked Maryann out of running away. She'd stay in school, wait until they both graduated, then they'd take off. They were tight now, always together. She didn't have to worry about her father anymore. Trash had straightened him out. Her father backed down, a coward at heart, took to his recliner and the TV, a few cool beers near at hand.

Trash made her stop taking things at the mall, or anywhere. "I know what it's like to be in jail," he said. "It's no party."

She didn't see Casey anymore. After her nervous breakdown, Casey stopped going to school. Maryann thought it was a little wimpy to go that far. Sure, she'd gotten hurt bad, but hadn't they both been there when he attacked them in the bathroom? If Maryann could come out of it okay, what was wrong with Casey? Not that she thought about it too much. She and Trash had plans for the future.

Sometimes Gena dreamed about the sound of his weeping. On those days she'd wake up sad. Sometimes she dreamed about the darkness, the feel of her lips on bloodied flesh, and she'd wake up screaming. The doctor prescribed pills. She was sick to her stomach a lot—lost almost fifteen pounds. She had a hard time eating and especially didn't want to see any meat on her plate. When Matt wanted a hamburger, he had to eat it on the deck, or at a fast-food place. She couldn't even stand to smell meat cooking, to see it in the refrigerator.

She saw Maryann in school but they never talked about the lake. They didn't hang out much, Maryann was always busy with her new boyfriend. Casey had lost it. Gena considered herself lucky—she knew she wasn't half as bad as Casey.

There were phone calls. At first everyone wanted to hear what happened. The kids wanted her to tell them all about the man-eating monster; they thought it was scary but cool. Reporters called too, especially that one that had been there when it happened, Megan McCauley. She had interviewed Gena for an exclusive story for her paper. But afterward, when other reporters asked, Gena refused to talk to them. Reliving it once was enough.

Then there were the sickies, calling and saying weird stuff, making jokes about chicken fingers. Her mother got an unlisted number and the calls stopped for a week, then started again. Sometimes they still got hang-ups. But not often enough for the police to get involved. Whoever it was never said anything anyway.

Gena knew it was her imagination, but she still felt something evil. She knew it couldn't be him, the man from the cellar, because she had seen him die. But she couldn't shake the feeling that something a lot like him was out there, perhaps even very close.

They were going to let him out soon. He'd been a good patient, cooperative, helpful, working hard toward his recovery. He did what he was told, smiled when it was appropriate, wore an earnest expression with his therapist.

They had no idea.

They asked him about his plans because it was important to go back to life with a plan. He talked about how he would get a GED since he had dropped out of school the year before. He even made noises about applying to college. He wasn't sure about a career yet, but they said that was okay, he had plenty of time. To make it all authentic and not too rosy, he made up a few bad dreams. Sometimes he looked sad and said, "Why me?"

"He's come through amazingly well," the doctor told his parents.

They had no idea how clever he could be.

He *did* have plans. Private plans. And they did not include a GED or college. He had better things to do when he was let out.

The phone calls were fun at first but got boring. Phil, one of the orderlies, who didn't give a shit so long as he could smoke on duty, let him use the phone at the nurse's desk at night. He got a real kick hearing the girl's shaky voice, or her mother—trying to sound tough. They changed their number, but he got Bailey to find out what the new one was. Bailey had turned into Mr. Good Guy, bringing flowers and candy to Gena, and coming to see him too.

But phone calls were not enough. He wanted hands-on. He liked that phrase: hands-on. He could hardly wait.

He might move somewhere else, or he might stay and have fun right here at home.

The door to his room opened and a nurse looked in. The blonde with the apple cheeks; he liked her.

"How's everything, Jeff?"

"Just fine," he answered.

"Good night, then," she replied softly. "Sleep tight."

Don't let the bedbugs bite. Bite bite bite. His mouth watered. He bit his tongue and tasted the blood. Good good good.

He slept and dreamed. The dark forest, the deep woods, beautiful places to hunt. The freedom of the night.

And the pleasure of the kill.

About The Author

Patricia Windsor is the author of sixteen novels and numerous short stories and articles. Her work has been translated into Norwegian, Danish, German, Afrikaans, Japanese, Hebrew, Italian, and French. She is a teacher, has worked in corporate public relations, has been both a magazine and a newspaper editor, and has spent time as a creative counselor in New York and London.

Patricia Windsor now lives in Maryland with her partner, Richard, and her cat, Annie Rose.